THE
YEAR
WITHOUT
MICHAEL

THE
YEAR
WITHOUT
MICHAEL

Susan Beth Pfeffer

F
Pfeffer

BANTAM BOOKS
TORONTO • NEW YORK • LONDON • SYDNEY • AUCKLAND

THE YEAR WITHOUT MICHAEL
A Bantam Book / September 1987
2nd printing January 1988

The Starfire logo is a registered trademark of Bantam Books,
a division of Bantam Doubleday Dell Publishing Group, Inc.
Registered in U.S. Patent and Trademark Office and elsewhere.

Library of Congress Cataloging-in-Publication Data

Pfeffer, Susan Beth, 1948–
　The year without Michael.

　Summary: The remaining members of the Chapman family try to cope with the
disappearance of fourteen-year-old Michael.
　[1. Missing persons—Fiction.　2. Family problems—Fiction]　I. Title.
PZ7.P44855Ye　1987　　[Fic]　87-11474
ISBN 0-553-05430-9

Bantam Books are published by Bantam Books, a division of Bantam Doubleday
Dell Publishing Group, Inc. Its trademark, consisting of the words "Bantam
Books" and the portrayal of a rooster, is Registered in U.S. Patent and
Trademark Office and in other countries. Marca Registrada. Bantam Books,
666 Fifth Avenue, New York, New York 10103.

PRINTED IN THE UNITED STATES OF AMERICA

FG　　11　10　9　8　7　6　5　4　3　2

For Liz Coleman

ACKNOWLEDGMENT

I wish to thank Pam Mather-Cathy for her assistance with this book.

Now, when I look back at that last evening, I see us all in a series of snapshots: my sister Kay's face illuminated by the kitchen light, hair pulled back with calculated disregard, doing her stretching exercises by the table. Michael, my brother, with that ever-present baseball cap perched cockily on the back of his head, grinning over the latest Mad magazine. Mom at the table, sipping her tea out of a mug, looking worried and trying not to act it. Even myself, thinking of nothing more serious than cheerleader tryouts, standing by the open kitchen door, looking over the backyard, staring at the sky, at the millions of stars, each casting its own light and history back to us, too simple to understand it.

AT FIRST

Sunday, September 1

They met at the front door.

"Where are you going?" Jody asked Michael.

"To Jerry's," he replied. "There's a softball game at his house. Want to come?"

Jody shook her head. "I'm meeting Maris at the movies," she said. "We're going to see *Tender Passions*."

Michael stuck his tongue out in disgust. "*Tender Passions*," he yelped. "Make me sick!"

"You make me sick," Jody declared. "You're such a baby sometimes. *Tender Passions* got very good reviews."

"Sure," Michael said. "And that's why you're going to see it. Not because it stars Dirk Whatshisname."

"Whitmore," Jody said. "Dirk Whitmore, and he has nothing to do with it." But she giggled.

"And don't call me baby anymore," Michael said. "I'll be in high school on Wednesday, same as you."

"You'll be a freshman," Jody reminded him. "It's hardly the same thing as being a junior. But I guess you are too big to call baby anymore." She smiled fondly at him.

Michael grinned back. "Where's Kay?" he asked.

"She and Mom went shopping for school clothes," Jody replied. "Kay outgrew all her things this summer, so Mom's doing a last minute job to get her a new wardrobe. They were fighting before they even got into the car."

"Mom had better spend her money fast," Michael said. "Get all new things while Dad's still around to pay for it."

"Don't talk that way," Jody said. "Dad isn't going anyplace."

"Yeah?" Michael said. "I don't exactly see him here this weekend."

"He's at the cabin," Jody said. "Thinking things out. That's not the same as asking for a divorce, you know."

3

"Maybe not yet," Michael said. "But that doesn't mean he isn't going to. He and Mom have been fighting less lately. That's a bad sign."

"What makes you think that?" Jody asked.

"I've watched my friends' parents," Michael said. "And lots of times right before they split up, they stop fighting. Because they know in their heads they're going to get divorced, so there's no point screaming anymore. They're saving all their screaming for court."

"I think you're crazy," Jody declared. "Mom and Dad have no intention of getting a divorce. They're working on saving their marriage. And just because Dad decided to get away for the weekend to think doesn't mean he's thinking about hiring a lawyer. A weekend away from us is probably all he needs to realize how much he'd miss us if he and Mom did split up."

Michael snorted. "Miss us?" he said. "You must be crazy. How could he miss Kay and her whining all the time, 'I'm not a baby anymore, stop treating me like I'm a baby'? And you always talking to that dumb Maris about boys."

"You still chew with your mouth open," Jody said. "You're disgusting sometimes, you know that, Michael."

"So you think Dad's going to want to stay here to teach me table manners?" Michael asked. "He's at the cabin right now packing his bags, thinking about the bachelor pad he's going to get the minute he works up his nerve to tell Mom he's leaving. And when that comes, you can kiss new wardrobes good-bye. I bet we'll even have to sell the house. Move to an apartment where they won't let us keep pets. We'll have to give Baron away to the Humane Society, and they'll gas him."

At the mention of his name, Baron walked over to Michael, rammed his head against Michael's ankle, and meowed. Michael opened the front door, and Baron ran out.

"Mom doesn't like it when you let Baron out through the front," Jody said.

"I won't tell her if you don't," Michael replied. "And Baron can keep a secret."

"Baron has more brains than you have," Jody said. "Even if Mom and Dad do split up, and I don't think they're going to,

4

that doesn't mean Dad's going to desert us. Sure, things'll be different, but we're not going to end up on welfare or anything."

"We'll never fit in an apartment," Michael declared. "Four of us in three and a half rooms. If you think things are bad with Kay now, think what it would be like sharing a room with her."

"You are absolutely crazy," Jody declared. "Go play some softball. Maybe you'll feel better after you've made a few errors."

"I don't make errors," Michael declared, opening the front door. "Enjoy your dumb movie."

"And don't be late for supper again," Jody called out to him, as Michael started walking toward Jerry's house. "Mom got real mad last time."

"I won't be late," Michael called back.

Jody stared at him and sighed. A lot of what Michael had said about their parents, she'd been thinking herself. But she'd been refusing to worry about it. Her parents were trying to save their marriage, and all she could do was hope that they succeeded.

She ran all the way to the movie theater and met Maris there. "I had to get out of the house," Maris declared as they stood on line for their tickets. "Mom's new boyfriend was driving me crazy."

"Your mom has a new new boyfriend?" Jody asked. "Or is this the one from last week?"

"New new," Maris said. "She met him Friday night. She says they met at the supermarket, but they both had liquor on their breath, so my guess is they met at Harpo's."

"Sounds like a fun guy," Jody said, conscious of the fact that everybody on line was listening to them. Maris never seemed to mind if the world knew her problems.

"They all are," Maris replied. "Could I stay at your house tonight? Mom'll probably come to her senses by tomorrow and he'll be gone. Her supermarket romances never last very long."

"I guess so," Jody said. "Just don't talk too much about your parents, okay? Mom's kind of sensitive these days about divorce talk."

"You think your parents are going to go through with it?" Maris asked. "Hello Divorce Court, Good-bye Daddy?"

"I don't know," Jody admitted. "I sure hope not."

"Well, even if they do, your mother isn't going to go crazy

like mine did," Maris said. "I can't picture your mother at a bar. She doesn't even drink, does she?"

"Just a little wine sometimes," Jody said. "Maris, I really don't want to talk about it."

"Okay," Maris said. "We'll talk about my mother instead. She spent half her last paycheck on bathing suits. Two bikinis, and two that might as well have been. All three sizes too small for her. I said, 'Mom, you can't fit in those, why did you buy them,' and she said 'They were great buys, they were all on sale.' And then she had the gall to say she'd meet a much nicer class of men hanging around the pool than she'd been able to at places like the supermarket. Like after she's through buying bathing suits that don't fit and going to Harpo's, she has enough money left for the supermarket. We ate nothing but peanut butter last week. Just peanut butter and crackers."

"You'll eat at our house tonight," Jody said. "One for *Tender Passions.*" She handed her money over to the ticket seller.

"One for *Tender Passions,*" Maris said. "Let's get a giant popcorn. I'm famished."

"Okay," Jody said. "But promise me you won't talk while the movie is on. It drives me crazy when you do that."

"Promise," Maris said. "But don't you hog the popcorn."

"Deal," Jody said, and soon the girls had settled in with their popcorn for an afternoon of relaxed lusting.

When they got back to Jody's house, her mother and Kay were unloading their purchases from the car. "Where's Michael?" Jody's mother asked, as Jody and Maris helped carry bags in.

"He's at Jerry Murphy's," Jody said. "Playing softball."

"Wanna see what I bought?" Kay asked in the kitchen.

"Sure," Jody said. "You get nice stuff?"

"Beautiful," Kay replied. "Mom wanted to get me all baby things, but I managed to convince her not to. Lookit."

"I'm looking," Jody said with a grin.

"Nice blouse, Kay," Maris said, picking it up and checking it out carefully. "Your mother has great taste."

"I picked that one out myself," Kay said. "Mom thought it was too old for me, but I knew it wasn't. I'm going into seventh grade after all. I can't keep dressing like I'm in kindergarten."

6

"I'm sick and tired of your complaining," Jody's mother declared. "All she did this afternoon was complain."

"Well, you kept picking ugly clothes," Kay replied. "Clothes we both knew would look lousy on me."

"Will you stop already," her mother said. "I swear that's the last time I'm taking you shopping."

Kay stuck her tongue out at her mother, but Jody was relieved to see her mother hadn't noticed. Maris did, though, and laughed. "Just like home," she said. "No wonder I always feel so comfortable here."

"Kay, take your new things and hang them up right now," her mother said.

"But I want to show them off," Kay said.

"You heard me," her mother said. "Now, before they all wrinkle and you start crying because they aren't perfect anymore."

Jody checked her mother out. "Maris and I are going upstairs," she said. "To listen to records. Okay?"

"Don't play them too loud," her mother said automatically, but then she looked at Jody and smiled. "I'll see you later," she said. "And I promise I'll be a human being again by suppertime."

"I'll hold you to it," Jody said. "Oh, Maris is staying for supper. Okay?"

"Sure," her mother said.

Jody and Maris went up to Jody's room. "I've seen your mother happier," Maris said.

"She's all right," Jody said. "Shopping with Kay could drive anyone crazy."

"Sure," Maris said. "Your mother's mood has nothing to do with your father."

"Could we please not talk about it?" Jody said. "Come on, Maris. I really want you to hear this album."

"Okay," Maris said. "I won't talk unless you want me to."

"Thank you," Jody said. She put the record on, and Maris actually did keep quiet. By the time Jody was ready to start talking again, both girls were more interested in the upcoming school year and *Tender Passions* than they were in Jody's parents.

"Jody!" her mother called upstairs.

Jody ran to the staircase. "What is it, Mom?"

7

"Where did you say Michael was?" her mother asked. "Supper's on the table."

"At Jerry's," Jody replied. "I told him to get back here for supper. I bet he forgot."

"I'll call him," her mother said. "Get Kay and Maris, would you, honey? We might as well start eating while the food is hot."

As the girls entered the kitchen, they could hear her mother on the phone. "Wait a second, Jerry," she was saying. "Are you sure about that?"

"What's up?" Jody asked.

"Jody, are you sure Michael went to Jerry's?" her mother asked.

Jody nodded. "To play softball."

"Jody says he was going to your house," Jody's mother said to Jerry. "Did anybody see him this afternoon? All right. Yes, Jerry, let me talk to your mother."

Jody and Kay exchanged glances. Maris merely looked puzzled.

"Hi, Anne," Jody's mother said. "Look, Jody says Michael was going to your house this afternoon to play softball, and Jerry says he never showed. Right. Jody, when did you see him last?"

"Around one," Jody said. "Maris and I met at the movies at one-fifteen, so it must have been right before then. He said he was going to Jerry's and I told him to be sure to get back here in time for supper. I watched him leave."

"Did you hear that, Anne?" Jody's mother asked. "Yes, I'd really appreciate that. Call if you hear anything. Thanks." She hung up the phone. "Anne's going to call the other kids at the game to see if any of them saw Michael," she declared. "Well, I suppose we might as well start supper." She put the food out on the table, but nobody began eating.

"Wait a second," Kay said. "I just remembered. Richard Keely called Michael this morning to see if he wanted to go to the movies. I bet Michael changed his mind and went there."

"The movies," her mother said, checking the clock. "It's already after six. You'd think he'd be home by now."

"Maybe he decided to have supper at Richard's," Kay said.

"I'll call," Jody's mother said, getting up and checking the number in the phone book. "Hello, Mrs. Keely? This is Linda

8

Chapman, Michael's mother. Yes, hello. Look, we seem to have misplaced Michael, and we thought maybe he'd gone to the movies with Richard. Could you ask him, please?" She stood there holding the phone for a moment, and then said, "He didn't see him at all? He's sure about that? Well, thank you. Yes, I'll call you as soon as we find him. Thanks again." She hung up the phone and stared out the back door. "Richard didn't see him," she said. "He says Michael told him he'd be going to Jerry's house."

"I bet he went to the cabin," Jody said. "To talk to Dad."

"How would he have gotten there?" Jody's mother asked.

"He could have biked to Uncle Rob's and asked for a lift," Jody replied.

"He could have even biked to the cabin himself," Kay said. "He did that once before last spring."

"He did?" Jody's mother asked. "He isn't supposed to. That highway is no place for bicycles."

"He didn't want you to know," Kay said. "But he did it once, so he might have done it this time."

"Kay, go to the garage and check to see if his bike is missing," her mother said. "I swear I'm going to kill him the moment he walks through the door. Jody, are you sure he said he was going to Jerry's house?"

"Positive," Jody said. "But he might have changed his mind. Michael was talking about Dad before he left, so maybe he did decide to go over there. Even if he biked, he probably figured Dad would give him a lift back."

"His bike's in the garage," Kay said, running back into the kitchen. "Mom, his bike is still there."

"I'm calling Rob," her mother said. "Jody, go into Michael's room and see if anything's missing."

"Okay, Mom," Jody said. Maris accompanied her upstairs.

"What are we looking for?" Maris asked.

"I don't know," Jody replied. "I guess we're looking for Michael."

"He's probably asleep in his bedroom," Maris said. "I saw that on a *Leave It to Beaver* once. Everybody got hysterical thinking Beaver had run away, but all the time he was asleep in his room."

"Michael didn't run away," Jody said, but she ran the few feet down the hall to Michael's room, hoping to find him lying on his bed. But he wasn't there. His room looked the way it always did, as though it had recently been hit by a tornado.

"How are you supposed to know if anything's missing?" Maris asked. "Michael could be right here, and you couldn't find him under all this mess."

"His wallet is here," Jody said, finding it on his chest of drawers. "But there's no money in it."

"Does he usually keep money in it?" Maris asked.

"I don't know," Jody admitted. "Maybe a couple of dollars."

"He isn't under the bed," Maris said, looking under there. "I saw that on a *Father Knows Best* episode once. Mom makes me watch all those shows on cable. She says they can provide me with a sense of stability."

"Maybe he's at Uncle Rob's," Jody said. "I'm going back downstairs."

"Fine," Maris said. "I'll look around upstairs. He might be hiding in a closet. I saw that on *My Three Sons*."

Jody flew downstairs and back to the kitchen. Her mother was just hanging up the phone.

"Rob hasn't heard from him," she said. "He's driving to the cabin now, to see if Michael's there."

"He didn't leave any note in his room," Jody said. "His wallet's there, but there isn't any money in it."

Jody's mother looked at her watch again. "He should have been here a half an hour ago," she said. "And nobody seems to have seen him since one. Are you sure he said he was going to Jerry's?"

Jody sighed. "I saw him leave for there," she said. "And he promised he'd be back in time for supper."

Out of nowhere a stereo started blasting.

"Michael," Jody's mother said.

"Maris," Jody said, and ran to the foot of the stairs. "Maris, turn the stereo off!" she shouted.

"Okay," Maris shouted back, and the music stopped as quickly as it had started. Maris walked downstairs. "No word, huh?" she said.

Jody shook her head.

"I'll check around the neighborhood," Maris said. "Maybe Michael fell asleep under a tree somewhere. I saw that on *The Andy Griffith Show* once."

"Thanks, Maris," Jody's mother said.

Maris left through the back door, and Baron came in. Jody bent down to pet the cat, and as she did the phone rang.

Jody grabbed it. "Oh hi, Mrs. Murphy," she said. "Did you find out anything?"

"I spoke to a half dozen of the kids," Anne Murphy replied. "All the ones who were here at one, and none of them saw Michael. David Greeley said he spoke to Michael around twelve and Michael said he'd see him here."

"Oh," Jody said. "That doesn't sound good."

"What?" her mother asked.

"Nothing," Jody said. "None of the other kids saw Michael."

"I sent Jerry out looking for him," Anne Murphy declared. "And Debbie Liebowitz and Connie Rossetti both said they'd drive around looking for him."

"That's great," Jody said. "Thank you."

"There are just so many horror stories," Anne said. "Call if you hear anything. And tell your mother we're scouting around for him."

"I will," Jody said. "Thanks again." She hung up the phone and told her mother what Anne had said.

"I'm going looking too," Kay said.

"No," her mother said sharply. "You stay here, Kay. I'm going to call the police. If there's been an accident somewhere, they'll know. I should have called them right away." She dialed the number and said, "My son Michael is missing. Please let me speak to a police officer."

"I want to look for Michael," Kay said.

"Kay, shut up," Jody said, and grabbed her sister. She pulled Kay out of the kitchen and into the living room.

"I want to look," Kay said.

"Fine," Jody said. "We'll look together. But let Mom talk to the police first. Maybe they know something."

"You don't think he was hurt, do you?" Kay asked.

"I don't know," Jody said. "I don't know what's happened."

Kay looked as though she were about to start crying. They

11

stood silently in the living room until they could hear their mother hang up the phone. Then Jody led Kay back into the kitchen.

"There were no accidents," Jody's mother said. "The police say it's probably nothing to worry about, but they think combing the neighborhood is a good idea."

"I'll start looking," Jody said. "Kay, stay with Mom, and keep her company."

"Thanks," Jody's mother said. "Come on, Kay. One of us might as well eat."

"I'm not hungry," Kay protested, but she sat down at the table, and at least tried to eat. Jody grinned at her and went to the garage to get her bike. She had no idea where to look, and even less of an idea where other people might have looked already. But it felt good to get away, to be doing something.

Jody biked around looking until after seven. She didn't see Michael, but she did notice a lot of other people out there looking for him also.

When she got home, she was tremendously relieved to find her father's car parked in the driveway. She ran her bike into the garage, and then sprinted to the kitchen. "Daddy!" she cried, and rushed into his arms. "Is Michael with you? Did you hear from him?"

"No, honey," her father said. "No word from Michael."

"But I thought he'd be at the cabin," Jody said. "I was sure of it. Where else would he have gone?"

"We don't know," her father said. "Rob is waiting there, just in case Michael does show up. Jody, I'd like you to meet Officer Dino. Officer Dino, this is my daughter Jody."

Jody looked at the police officer. It felt strange seeing an officer in uniform sitting in her kitchen, but everything felt strange by then. She noticed her mother standing by the refrigerator, and Kay hovering in the doorway.

"Hello, Jody," Officer Dino said. "I was just finding out as much as I could about Michael."

"He's thirteen," Jody's mother said.

"He's almost fourteen," Kay said. "His birthday's in two weeks."

"And he's about five foot two," Jody's mother continued.

12

"Maybe five three. He's grown a little bit this summer, but not as much as he'd like. He weighs, oh, I don't know, a hundred, a hundred ten. He's a little small for his age."

"We have pictures," Jody's father said. "In case you need them. I took a bunch of snapshots over the Fourth of July."

"Good," Officer Dino said. "I will take a couple, just to be on the safe side. Now, Jody, your mother tells me you were the last person to see Michael this afternoon."

Jody nodded. "Around one," she said. "He told me he was going to Jerry Murphy's house to play softball."

"Did you and your brother talk about anything else?" Officer Dino asked. "Can you remember anything Michael might have said that would indicate where he could have gone off to?"

Jody shook her head. "He was going to Jerry's," she said. "I told him not to be late for supper, and he said he wouldn't be."

"And what time is supper?" Officer Dino asked.

"Six," Jody replied.

Officer Dino checked his watch. "So he's been missing for a little over an hour," he declared.

"But nobody's seen him since one," Jody's mother cried.

"I understand that," Dino said. "And I certainly understand your concern. But it's too soon to panic. Now, Jody, just what did you and Michael talk about?"

"Nothing," Jody said. "Just stuff."

Dino smiled. " 'Stuff' covers a lot of ground," he said. "Did you two talk about anything in particular?"

"Mostly family," Jody said, blushing. "Family stuff."

"Oh, family stuff," Dino said. "Like what?"

"Nothing important," Jody said. "Just about how Dad was at the cabin this weekend."

Officer Dino cleared his throat. "You all look like very nice people," he said. "And this must be a very difficult time for you, having me sit in your kitchen while you're worried about your son. But if there are any problems in this family, it's going to make looking for Michael a lot easier if the police know just what's going on. Assuming we have to look for him."

"I went away for the weekend to do some thinking about our marriage," Jody's father said. "Linda was going to do the same thing right here. That's all. We're not talking about divorce."

13

"But there are problems," Dino said. "Is that what you and Michael were talking about, Jody? Your parents' marriage?"

Jody nodded.

"Sure," Dino said. "Kids pick up on things, worry all the time. My wife and I have a little fight, the kids are always after us, asking if we're getting a divorce. There's so much of it around, you can't blame them for wondering. Michael was maybe concerned your folks were splitting up, right, Jody?"

"I said they weren't going to," Jody said. "And he said he was going to Jerry's."

"Did he mention anything about running away?" Dino asked.

"Michael wouldn't run away," Jody's mother said. "He's not the kind of boy to run away from his problems."

"He wouldn't see it that way," Dino replied. "He'd see it as solving a problem, not avoiding one. Jody, you spoke to him last. Do you think Michael might have decided to run away?"

"I don't know," Jody said. "I don't think so. He was worried about Dad, we all are, but he didn't sound worried. And he certainly didn't say anything about single-handedly saving the marriage. It sounded more like he was sure they were going to get divorced, and he was worried about how we'd all make out afterwards."

"My God," Jody's father said. "I never realized how concerned you kids were."

Kay started crying in the doorway.

"I think it's a good idea for the neighbors to keep a lookout for Michael," Dino said. "And if he isn't home by dark, we'll get a more organized search going. But let me assure you, most runaways show up within a day. They realize life isn't so much fun without a bed to sleep on and a mother to make them breakfast, and they come right home."

"But what if he isn't a runaway?" Jody's father asked.

"I'll tell you the truth, Mr. Chapman," Dino declared. "If Michael were just two weeks older, if he were already fourteen, instead of just going on fourteen, I wouldn't even be here. The police automatically assume any kid fourteen or over who's not where he's supposed to be is a runaway. And this seems like a runaway situation. There are problems in the family, the school year is just about to start. Things get to be a little too much for

14

him, he decides to take some of the pressure off, maybe make his parents worry about him. Kids do it all the time. He'll probably be home by bedtime, full of adventures to tell you."

"What if he isn't?" Jody's father said. "What if something else happened to him?"

"Folks, you'd rather think he was a runaway," Dino said. "If you're going to worry, and of course you are, you might as well worry about something that'll have a happy ending."

"I don't understand," Jody said. "What else could have happened?"

"Lots of things," Dino said. "None of them pretty, and none of them likely, thank God."

"But those things do happen," Jody's mother said. "I read about them all the time. Abductions by strangers. Little children just vanishing on the streets. Paper boys, kids Michael's age."

"Mrs. Chapman, I'm not going to lie to you," Officer Dino said. "Yes, those things do happen. But the very fact that you read about them shows how rare it is. Most missing kids are either runaways or taken by noncustodial parents. Very, very few kids just vanish."

"But what if Michael is one of them?" Jody's mother asked. "What then?"

Dino scratched his head. "If Michael doesn't come home soon, we'll organize the neighborhood, get everybody out there looking for him. If he doesn't come home by tomorrow morning, then we'll treat him as a missing persons case, put out an APB on him. You can run off handouts, posters, get them put in the stores in the area, so people will know to look for him. Meanwhile, why don't you make lists of people Michael might have contacted. His grandparents maybe, or old friends who might have moved away from the neighborhood. Start making phone calls, and see if one of them turns up your boy."

"I haven't called his grandparents because I didn't want them to worry," Jody's mother said. "But Michael is close to your father, Tom. Maybe he did contact them."

"Start calling," Dino said. "Meanwhile, I'll start driving around the outskirts of town, see if I can locate him. You promised me some pictures."

"Here," Jody's father said, taking a couple from his wallet. "This one is real good."

"Yeah, it's fine," Dino said. "Nice-looking boy. I have a twelve-year-old daughter who'd say he's real cute. Okay, folks, I'll be back here in a little while to see if there's any word. Meantime, try not to worry."

"Thank you," Jody's father said. Officer Dino left by the back door, and Jody's mother walked over to the phone. "I hate to call," she said. "In case Michael tries to call us, and gets a busy signal."

"If it's an emergency, he'll break through," Jody's father said. "Remember when my mother did that last year? Michael was the one on the phone, so he knows it can be done."

"I just wish I knew where he was," Jody's mother said.

"I'm going out again," Jody said. "To look for him. Kay, you want to come with me?"

"Yeah," Kay said. "Mom, can we?"

"Just be back before dark," her mother replied. "I don't want to lose all of you in one day."

"We'll be back in half an hour," Jody said. "Promise. Come on, Kay." She and her sister walked out the back door, and started to stroll away from their house.

"Where are we going?" Kay asked after they'd walked half a block.

"I don't know," Jody admitted. "I just had to get out of there. Mom looks terrible."

"She was crying until Dad got home," Kay said. "Dad looked real mad, and then he started crying too, and then Officer Dino came in. Do you think Michael ran away?"

"I don't know what to think," Jody said. "Did Michael say anything to you about running away?"

Kay shook her head. "I don't think he was scared about school starting either," she declared. "He was teasing me about it yesterday, about how I was still a little kid, going to middle school, but he was a big kid in high school already."

"Yeah, I know," Jody said. "He never mentioned being scared to me."

"What if Michael was kidnapped?" Kay asked. "We're not rich. We can't afford a ransom."

"I don't think if Michael was kidnapped, it would be like that," Jody said, and her throat constricted. "You know all those

16

talks they've had at school lately, about how you should be careful with strangers, and what to do if anybody tries to grab you?"

"They do that with boys too?" Kay asked. "All that sex stuff?"

Jody nodded.

"You mean somebody might have taken Michael for that?" Kay asked. "Like rape or something?"

"I'm sure that isn't what's happened," Jody said. "It's probably more like Maris was saying. Michael just fell asleep somewhere and he'll wake up when he gets hungry."

"Sometimes they murder kids," Kay said. "I remember last spring, it was on all the news shows, and all the kids were talking about it. Some girl got raped and murdered maybe a hundred miles from here. Remember, Mom was worried until they caught the man they said did it. She was only ten and he murdered her."

"Nobody's murdered Michael," Jody said. "And don't you even suggest that to Mom or Dad. They have enough to worry about right now."

"Do you think they're thinking it though?" Kay asked. "That maybe Michael's been raped or murdered?"

"They're thinking it," Jody said. "If we're thinking it, they're thinking it. But that doesn't mean it happened. Michael's only been missing for a few hours. And Officer Dino doesn't think that's what happened at all, and he sounds like he has a lot of experience in these things."

"If Michael was murdered, they'll find his body, right?" Kay said.

"Michael wasn't murdered," Jody declared.

"Then where is he?" Kay asked.

"I don't know," Jody cried. "None of us know, dammit. If we knew, we wouldn't all be worrying, now would we?"

"I'm sorry," Kay said. "I'm just scared."

"I know," Jody said. "I'm scared too. I'm so scared it's like all my insides are just floating around bumping into each other. Michael's been missing for over six hours now, and I don't think Officer Dino realizes it. And it isn't like Michael to run away. He's never run away before, and he didn't say anything to me that sounded like he was about to. Only we can't think anything

17

really awful has happened to him, because we don't know, and it'll just drive us crazy if we do. And Michael could come home in ten minutes, and laugh at all of us for worrying so much."

"I hope so," Kay said. "What are we going to do if he doesn't?"

Jody looked away from Kay, and stared at the elm trees down the block. "Then we'll start worrying," she said. "And we'll have to be as strong as we know how, stronger even, until Michael comes home. Because he will come home. Even if he did something dumb like run away, he'll come home."

"And if he was kidnapped?"

"Then he'll figure out a way of escaping," Jody said. "And he'll come home. Or the police will find him and bring him home."

"And if he was murdered?"

"He wasn't murdered," Jody declared. "That only happens on television. Kay, he didn't say anything to you, did he, about where he might have gone? Something you wouldn't want Mom or Dad to know about?"

Kay shook her head. "We had a fight this morning about the telephone," she said. "He was on it and I wanted to use it and he teased me about being on the phone all the time. That was it."

"There's Maris," Jody said. "Maris, we're over here."

Maris trotted over to them. "Any word from Michael?" she asked.

"Not yet," Jody said. "The police sent a man over, and he's out looking now. He says we shouldn't worry."

"The cops always say that," Maris declared. "They don't care what happens. Do you want me to keep looking?"

"If you want to," Jody replied. "Would you mind not coming back to our house? I don't think Mom can handle any company right now, not even you."

"Okay," Maris said. "Call me if you hear anything."

"Of course," Jody said. "Thanks, Maris."

"Any time," Maris said, and began the walk back to her home. Jody watched as Maris walked away, and almost called out to her to come back, but she knew she shouldn't.

"If Mom and Dad do split up, is Mom going to act like Maris's mother?" Kay asked.

"Never," Jody said. "That's the one thing you can count on."

"Good," Kay said. "Do you think Michael is home yet?"

"If he isn't, I'm sure he'll be home real soon," Jody replied.

"If I have stuff to worry about, can I ask you?" Kay said. "Stuff about Michael, maybe, or Mom and Dad. Not baby stuff, but things to worry about, you know."

"I know," Jody said, and put her arm around Kay's shoulders. "Of course you can. That's what big sisters are for."

"And you can talk to me too," Kay said. "That's what little sisters are for."

"I'm glad to hear it," Jody said. "Come on, let's get home before the whole neighborhood starts searching for us."

Their mother was still on the phone when they got back, and their father had taken the car and was driving around. The sun set, the moon came out, and at eight-thirty Officer Dino dropped by.

"We have several men out looking for Michael," he declared. "We're still sure he'll be home by bedtime, but there's no point taking any chances."

"He's been missing for almost eight hours," Jody's mother said.

"That's one way of looking at it," Dino replied. "Or you could say he's been missing for a couple of hours, a little more. I think you'll be happier if you think of it that way."

"I'm not going to be happy about anything until we find him," Jody's mother declared. "I don't care if he's been missing for eight hours or eight minutes. I want to know where my son is, and I want the police department to do everything they can to find him."

"We're doing everything in our power, Mrs. Chapman," Dino replied. "And let me assure you once again that ninety-nine and nine tenths of these situations wind up with happy endings. If I were a betting man, I'd bet that you'll be fixing Michael a hearty breakfast tomorrow morning."

"I just pray that you're right," Jody's mother said. "But if you aren't, you'd better be doing everything humanly possible to find my son."

"We will be," Dino said. "Now let me go back out and see

19

what I can find. It'd be my pleasure to bring Michael home to you."

"I hate him," Jody's mother declared as soon as Dino had left the house. "I know I shouldn't, but if he hands me one more platitude, I swear I'm going to scream."

"I don't feel so good," Kay said. "Mom, can I go to bed now?"

"Of course, honey," her mother replied. "You know, you hardly touched your supper. Would you feel better if you ate something?"

"I don't think so," she said. "Maybe later, when Michael gets home."

"Fine," her mother said. "Call me if you need anything." She walked over to Kay and gave her a kiss and a hug.

" 'Night," Kay said, and walked upstairs. Jody almost followed her, but she didn't know what to say, so she stayed behind with her mother.

The house seemed unusually quiet then, no TV on, no after-dinner noises. Jody could hear the birds and the crickets outside, and the sound of cars driving by. More cars than usual, she realized. Probably people driving around looking for Michael.

"He'll be all right," she said to her mother, she said to herself.

"I know," her mother said. "Come on, let's make some sandwiches. Even if we're not hungry, other people will be."

Jody followed her mother into the kitchen, and soon the two of them were making tuna salad sandwiches, and peanut butter and jelly sandwiches, and roast beef sandwiches. They worked in silence, making sandwich after sandwich until they had used up close to two loaves of bread.

"There isn't enough milk," Jody's mother said, staring at the sandwiches. "What if people come over, and they want milk with their sandwiches?" And standing there, at the kitchen counter, she began to cry.

"Mom, it'll be okay," Jody said. "We have other things for them to drink. Nobody drinks milk nowadays anyway."

Her mother stared at her for a moment, laughed, and then started crying again, only harder this time.

"Oh Jody," her mother said. "Jody, I'm so scared."

"I know," Jody said, and she patted her mother on the back, the way her mother always patted her when she was the one sobbing. "Mom, he'll be back, I promise you. He'll be back. He'll be back home soon."

Monday, September 2

She didn't fall asleep until close to four o'clock, and by a quarter after six she was wide awake. Jody put on the clothes she'd been wearing the day before and tiptoed downstairs. Her parents had fallen asleep on the living room sofa, her mother's head resting on her father's lap. Jody moved as quietly as she could into the kitchen. Most of the sandwiches were gone, but she found half a peanut butter and jelly left, and she devoured it. She knew she'd eaten the night before, she remembered sandwich after sandwich being chewed and swallowed, but she was absolutely famished, as though she had never eaten in her life.

There was a note from Kay on the kitchen table. "I woke up early and went out to look for Michael," she'd scribbled. She hadn't put a time down, but Jody suspected Kay had left a few minutes earlier. That was probably what had waked her.

The phone rang. Jody jumped up, feeling as though a bullet had just pierced her heart. She ran over to it, and whispered "Hello."

"This is Granny," Jody's grandmother said. "Jody, is that you?"

"Yes, Gran," Jody said.

"Is there any word yet?" her grandmother asked. "I've been sitting by the phone all night waiting to hear."

"There's nothing to tell you, Gran," Jody replied. "Michael still isn't home."

"Let me speak to your father," her grandmother said. "Is he there or is he out looking?"

21

"He's asleep," Jody said.

"No I'm not," her father declared, walking into the kitchen. "I'll take that. Hello, Mom," he said into the phone. "No, Linda and I were up almost all night, and there's no word. Yes, the police have organized the search. They're going to comb the woods around town this morning, but they don't think they'll find anything. Yes, that's what they still think, that he ran away. But we haven't heard anything yet."

Jody left the kitchen and walked back to the living room. Her mother was straightening herself out on the sofa, patting her hair, tugging her shirt under her waistband. "It's Gran," Jody told her.

"It would be," her mother replied. "We begged her not to call, but I guess she couldn't hold out."

"Dad says they're going to search the woods," Jody said.

"And do a door-to-door search in the neighborhood," her mother declared.

"They think Michael is being held prisoner right here?" Jody asked.

Her mother shook her head. "They think he ran away," she replied. "And at this point, I'm praying that's what happened. But on the off chance he didn't, somebody might have seen something, Michael walking somewhere or on the road hitching. Rob's going to check out the area around the cabin, just in case Michael did go in that direction."

"Kay is out looking," Jody said. "She left a note."

Her mother sighed. "What Kay thinks she's going to find is beyond me," she said. "But I guess she needs to feel useful."

"I'd like to feel useful too," Jody said. "What can I do?"

"You can give me a hug," her mother said, and Jody obliged. "I don't know, Jody. I just don't know. Michael isn't the kind of boy to scare us this way. He's never been irresponsible, none of my children are. But if he hasn't run away, then . . . then God only knows what may have become of him. And I can't handle that right now."

"I'm making coffee," Jody's father called from the kitchen. "Linda, you want some?"

"I might as well," she replied, getting up. "My nerves are so jangled, the coffee can't possibly hurt."

Within ten minutes, the house had filled up with people. Neighbors had come bringing breads and coffee cakes, and Officer Dino had arrived with a couple of other police officers.

"We'd like to take Jody and Kay to the station, if we could," Dino said. "We'd like them to look over some mug shots to see if they recognize any faces."

"I don't understand," Jody said. "Whose mug shots? What are we looking for?"

"They're known sex offenders," Dino replied. "Ones who live in roughly a hundred-mile radius of here. You or Kay might have spotted one of them near your school, or in your neighborhood, or even possibly talking to Michael. It's a long shot, but we don't have much to go on, so it's worth the chance."

"Kay's out looking," Jody said.

"As soon as she comes back in, I'll have someone take her to the station," Jody's mother declared. "Honey, please go even if it's hard. Maybe you'll recognize someone."

"All right," Jody said. It felt extremely odd going with a police officer in a squad car and driving away from her house. She felt guilty somehow, although she couldn't be sure what she was guilty of. Letting Michael disappear, she suspected. She should have said something to keep him from leaving the house. She should have agreed to go to the Murphys' instead of meeting Maris at the movies. There must have been something she could have done differently that would have prevented all this from happening.

"It's rough when a kid disappears," the officer said.

"Yeah," Jody said. "It's rough."

The police station was a scene of controlled bedlam. "Things are a little busier here than usual," the police officer told Jody. "Labor Day weekend, things are always heavy, more crime, more drownings, lot more car accidents. And of course a lot of the guys came out to help look for Michael. Janet, do you have the books ready?"

"Ready," an officer replied. "Hello, Jody. My name is Janet Dreiser, and I have the mug books for you to look through. Did Officer Dino explain what we wanted you to look for?"

"Yes, he did," Jody said. "I really don't remember seeing Michael talking to anyone unusual lately."

"We understand that," Officer Dreiser replied. "But a face may jog a memory. And it could be someone who didn't speak to Michael, but who's been hanging around the school yards. We need to check it out."

"Sure," Jody said. "At least I'll feel like I'm doing something to help."

"Make yourself comfortable," Officer Dreiser said. "Here are the books." She placed three large books on a table in front of Jody.

"I'm supposed to look through all these?" Jody asked.

"As many as you can manage," Officer Dreiser replied. "Take your time. And if you think you recognize anybody, let me know. I'll be right over here."

"Thank you," Jody said.

"Would you like something to eat or drink?" Officer Dreiser asked. "Have you had breakfast?"

"Not just now, thank you," Jody replied. "Maybe later."

"Give me a holler when you want something," the police officer said. "And if you have any questions, just ask."

"Sure," Jody said, and began the task of looking through the pictures. It was terrifying seeing how many sex offenders there were in the area. At first each picture looked different, each face having its own wretched story to tell. But after half an hour, forty-five minutes, an hour of looking at face after face, they all melted into one. Jody pushed the book away, and covered her eyes with her hands.

"Had enough for now?" Officer Dreiser asked.

"I can't stand it anymore," Jody said, and she found herself crying on Officer Dreiser's shoulder. "I can't. Nobody looks familiar. I don't know any of those men. Where's Michael? I want Michael."

"I know, I know," Officer Dreiser said. "Oh look, this must be your sister. She can take over for you for a little while."

"I don't want her to see me crying," Jody said, and she inhaled deeply, while wiping her tears away with her hand. "Hi, Kay," she said. "Any word?"

"Nothing," Kay said. "I feel like I'm under arrest." She laughed nervously.

"They're very nice here," Jody said. "If you're hungry, Kay, they'll get you something to eat."

"I'm not hungry," Kay replied. "Granny and Granddad wanted to come, and Dad got into a big fight with them on the phone, telling them to stay where they are. In case Michael tries to call them. And people keep coming in, bringing us food, and then they eat what everybody else brought. It's like a party back there. And there are reporters too, outside the house, and they keep asking what Michael was like. Only they ask it like he's dead."

"He isn't dead," Jody said automatically. She wondered at what point she'd stopped being so sure. "The police will find him soon. Or else he'll call. For all we know, he's calling right now."

"Jerry Murphy was on the radio," Kay said. "He said Michael was the best infielder they had." She began to cry softly, and Jody ran over to her.

"Don't cry," Jody whispered. "If you cry, then I'll start crying too, and we'll flood this place with our tears."

Kay looked up at Jody and sniffled. "Is that a joke?" she asked.

"I don't think so," Jody replied. "I don't think I have any jokes left inside me."

"Come here, Kay," Officer Dreiser said. "Your sister has already looked through these pictures, so if you could just start here? Let me know if anybody looks familiar to you."

"All right," Kay said.

"Can I go home now?" Jody asked. It was getting harder and harder to breathe the air in the police station.

"Certainly," Officer Dreiser said. "We'll give you a lift right now. I'll take care of your sister."

"I'd rather walk," Jody said.

Officer Dreiser pursed her lips. "We'd really prefer to drive you home," she said. "We don't want anything happening to you on your way."

"I need to walk," Jody said. "I'll be fine, honest."

"We'll have one of our officers drive behind you," Officer Dreiser said. "How's that for a compromise?"

"Fine," Jody said with a sigh. She gave Kay a kiss good-bye, and walked out of the station. The sun was shining, there were no clouds in the sky, and the temperature felt like it was about seventy-five. A perfect Labor Day. A perfect end-to-summer day.

She began walking, and then her walk turned into a jog, and the jog became a sprint. She felt like a fool having the police car right behind her, but she needed to move, to be outdoors, to be in an unenclosed space. Where was Michael? she thought, and realized that was the first time she'd actually asked herself that question. Where was he? Was he in an unenclosed space, or was he tied up somewhere, being held prisoner by one of those mug-shot faces she'd been unable to identify? Was he in the city, walking around, unaware of the pain he was causing, or maybe somehow sensing it, and enjoying the power he held over his family, his community? Or was he lying in a ditch somewhere, buried under a pile of leaves, thrown into a lake, a river, no longer Michael, but a Michaelbody, a cold stiff mass of flesh, shot, strangled, knifed, mutilated?

Jody stopped running and stood on the sidewalk, her body shaking uncontrollably. The police car pulled over to her side, and the officer stuck his head out. "You okay?" he asked.

"Have they found any bodies?" Jody asked.

"No," the officer said. "No bodies."

"Then he's alive?" Jody said, but it came out like a question. "He must be alive?"

"We sure hope so," the police officer said. "I mean, we're sure he is."

"I don't think I can walk any more," Jody said. "Could you drive me the rest of the way?"

"No problem," the officer said, opening the door for her. It was only two more blocks, but Jody didn't care. Her legs could no longer support her body. Her mind could no longer support her thoughts. She sat in the car, and cried in front of another uniformed stranger.

When she had calmed down, the officer dropped her off at her house. Jody hated the thought of walking in, but knew she had no choice in the matter. Her parents needed her, and she couldn't let them down.

"Thank goodness you're back," her mother said. "Maris is in the kitchen, and she insists on talking with you."

"Maris?" Jody said. There were people all over the living room—family, friends, neighbors, police officers, reporters, a mass of people who had never met Michael or heard of him, who

26

were now in her home, eating, smoking, behaving as though it were the most natural thing to be there. Jody recognized Michael's eighth-grade English teacher, and the assistant principal of the middle school. People were setting up committees, flyers were being handed out.

"They've already printed these up," her mother said, waving a flyer. "Mr. Hodgkins came in early this morning, and printed them up at his shop. Everybody's been so wonderful. There are a hundred people looking through the woods, and Rob says there are almost that many looking near the cabin. Boy Scouts. And the police, of course. Police dogs too. And the police in the city have been notified, in case Michael shows up there. At the bus terminal or the train station. Lots of kids run away on Labor Day weekend, because summer's ending, and the school year's about to begin. Not that I think he's there. I think he's probably someplace none of us have thought to check, someplace safe, and he's probably feeling a little foolish by now, and that's the only reason he hasn't called us. He knows he's all right, and he knows how angry we must be, and maybe he isn't ready just yet to crawl home, but any moment now, the phone will ring, and it will be Michael asking for a lift back home. The phone will ring, and it will be him, and oh, we'll let him know how angry we are, but then we'll laugh and cry and everybody will leave our house, and the nightmare will be over. That's what's going to happen. Everyone will blame me for causing such a fuss, but that won't matter because I'll have my son back, Michael will be back."

"Yes, Mama," Jody said.

"Go into the kitchen and talk to Maris," her mother said. "She's driving your father crazy."

"All right," Jody said. There was no point in asking her mother if she was all right. Obviously her mother wasn't, and there was nothing Jody could do to change that.

"Hi, Maris, what's up?" she asked, as she walked into the kitchen. The question sounded unbearably foolish to her, and she almost began to laugh, but didn't let herself. Laughter was as dangerous as tears.

"I need to talk to you," Maris said, grabbing Jody by the arm. "Let's go outside."

"Okay," Jody said, just as happy not to be in the house. They sat under the cherry tree toward the back of the yard. Jody could feel the house burning with activity even from that distance. People walked past the windows, phones rang, cars drove up, some cruising the block, some parking as close as they could. Doors opened and slammed shut. At that point, the house was more alive than Jody.

Baron walked over to the girls and curled up next to Jody. She patted him absently, and wondered if anybody had bothered to feed him.

"I had an awful night last night," Maris said. "I had to talk to you."

"None of us had a great night," Jody replied. "What happened to you?"

"The usual," Maris replied. "Mom. First she got drunk, and then she got ugly. I kept wishing I was here with you. But I knew I couldn't be. That made things worse."

"You couldn't have stayed here," Jody said. "We have problems of our own just now."

"Don't you think I know that?" Maris said. "Why do you think I came here today? Anyway, I locked myself in the bathroom until Mom came to her senses, which she did at dawn. I made us both some coffee and we sat around talking about Michael."

"Oh," Jody said. "Did your mother have any ideas?"

"Well, she's convinced Michael ran away," Maris replied. "I've been threatening to often enough lately. I swear I will too if she doesn't straighten out fast. And with your parents splitting up, Michael probably just wanted to get some attention, so he ran off."

"My parents are not splitting up," Jody said. "But all right. We're all hoping he ran away too."

"I can't say as I blame him," Maris said. "The way things are with Mom, I'm just about ready to run away myself. What do you think?"

Jody stared at Maris, and then stood up slowly. "You're asking me if you should run away?" she asked. "Michael has been missing since yesterday afternoon, and you're asking my permission to run away?"

"I don't need your permission," Maris said. "I only came here to help."

"Thank you, but we don't need your help," Jody said. "We don't need anybody's help. Everybody is here trying to help, and none of them are doing any good. Not the police, not the neighbors, not the reporters, not you. Nobody can help. Not until Michael comes home. I wish they'd all go away until then. I wish you'd go away too. I wish you'd all stay away until Michael comes home."

Tuesday, September 3

*T*hat morning Jody woke up, and there was no Michael. Baron was gone too, having refused to enter a house so full of activity and noise. Kay was still around though, sleeping in Jody's bed. And she could hear her parents, so she knew they hadn't disappeared overnight.

She looked at her watch and was startled to see it was close to ten. She couldn't remember when she'd fallen asleep the night before, but it had been late, she knew that. The house hadn't cleared of people until after midnight.

Jody threw on a robe, not caring that there could well be strangers downstairs. She didn't have the energy to look for clean clothes quietly enough not to disturb Kay. The world had seen what the Chapman family looked like at their worst moment. Now it could see what she looked like in a robe.

There were a few people downstairs, but it was nothing like the mob scene the day before. Of course not, she realized, as she grabbed a piece of coffee cake. Monday had been Labor Day, and people hadn't had to go to work. Today was just an average Tuesday, and there was no time for other people's crises.

"Any news?" she asked her father, who was drinking yet another cup of coffee.

"As a matter of fact, there might be," he said. "The police found a woman this morning who lives over on Willow Street, about seven blocks from here, and she says she saw a boy around Michael's age talking to a strange man in a car Sunday afternoon."

"You're kidding," Jody said. "That's great. Did she recognize Michael from his pictures?"

"She said she couldn't be sure," her father replied. "She just happened to glance out the window and notice the two of them. Then she went away for Labor Day, and she didn't think anything of it until she read the paper this morning and saw the article about Michael. She called the police herself to tell them."

"What would Michael have been doing on Willow Street?" Jody asked. "He was going to Jerry's when I talked to him, and Willow's in the opposite direction."

"I know," her father said. "We pointed that out to the police. They think if it was Michael, then there's probably some simple explanation for it. Maybe he decided to buy some gum or he remembered he wanted to talk to a friend of his. Or maybe he just got distracted, and walked away without even thinking about it."

"Did Michael . . . did the boy look scared?" Jody asked. "Could she recognize the man? What about his car?"

"She said the boy didn't seem scared to her. If she had suspected something was wrong, she would have gone out to check," Jody's father replied. "Or at least that's what she thinks now. She didn't get that much of a look at the man, because he was in the car, and she didn't know he might be a suspect someday. And the car was a two-door hatchback of some kind, brown, she thought, or maybe tan."

"That's not much to go on," Jody said.

"No," her father agreed. "But it's all we have for the moment."

"Where's Mom?" Jody asked.

"Upstairs asleep," her father replied. "She finally took the sedative Dr. Mueller gave her, and she's going to be out for a while. She needs the sleep." He kneaded the back of his neck absently. "I guess we all do."

"Kay's sleeping in my room," Jody said. "She didn't want to spend the night alone."

"I can't imagine what this is doing to her," Jody's father said. "To you either, for that matter. Well, tomorrow is the first day of school. And whether we've heard from Michael by then or not, the two of you will go and that will help."

"I'd rather stay home," Jody declared.

"I know," her father said. "But your mother and I will be a lot happier if you're in school. Besides, Officer Dino is convinced Michael will turn up today. He says a lot of runaways come to their senses after a couple of days. Especially when they realize they can still get back home before the school year begins. He's really very optimistic. As a matter of fact, we're under strict instructions that one of us should answer the phone today, just in case it is Michael. If he hears a strange voice, he might panic and hang up, but if we answer the phone, Dino seems to think, Michael will be all too happy to tell us where he is."

"I hope he's right," Jody said. "Dad, this isn't like Michael. He's such a worrier. When you're ten minutes late from work, he's convinced there's been an accident. And look at what he said on Sunday, all that talk about what our finances were going to be like just because you and Mom are having a few problems. I can't picture him running away for so long. I just can't, Dad. I try and I try, and it doesn't feel like Michael to me. Kay maybe, but not Michael."

"I know," her father said. "But it's our best hope. At this point, it's close to our only hope, and we need it to hold on to. Strange men in brown hatchbacks just aren't enough. Would you like some coffee?"

"You don't let me drink coffee," Jody said. "Remember, Dad?"

"Oh, that's right," he said. "I've offered so many people so many things the past couple of days I've lost track. You don't suppose that's why Michael left, do you? Because we said he was too young to drink coffee?"

"No, Dad," Jody said, and she realized with a flash that if her father broke down, she wouldn't be able to stand it. She could handle everything else, she thought, everything she had to, but only if she knew her father was all right. Without him, she

31

would have to take care of her mother and Kay and her grand-parents and the neighbors and the strangers and the pain. And she couldn't do it alone. Nobody should expect her to, she thought, feeling resentment. She wasn't the grown-up, why should she have to handle things?

"I'm all right," her father said in answer to her unspoken thoughts. "Just distracted, honey. Distracted and scared."

"I know," Jody said. "It's okay. It has to be."

"It does," her father said. "And who knows? Michael might walk through that door at any moment. As we're sitting here talking, he could be on his way home."

"I hope so, Dad," Jody said. "Oh God, how I hope so."

The telephone rang, and Jody nearly jumped out of her skin. "Unless it's Michael," her father said, and Jody nodded. She clenched and unclenched her fists and answered the phone.

"Jody, it's Lauren. I just heard."

"Lauren," Jody said. "When did you get home?"

"Last night," Lauren replied. "Late. And this morning I read the paper and saw the article about Michael. Have you heard anything?"

"Not yet," Jody replied. "And I shouldn't really stay on the phone, just in case he's trying to call."

"I understand," Lauren replied, and Jody, knowing that she did, felt better. "May I come over?"

"Please," Jody said. "See you later."

"I'm on my way," Lauren declared and hung up. Jody turned around and faced her father. "Lauren's back," she said. "I told her it was okay to come over."

"Fine," her father said. "Lauren's a nice girl. Levelheaded."

Unlike Maris, Jody thought with a smile. Lauren and Maris had been her two best friends for years now, and her parents had never hidden their preference. Maris was greeted with tolerant, occasionally sympathetic, smiles. Lauren received genuine warmth.

Jody bent over and gave her father a kiss on his forehead. He looked up at her and smiled. "You've been terrific," he said. "Your mom and I really appreciate it."

"It's okay," Jody said.

"When Michael gets back, we'll work out our problems together," her father declared. "That's a promise. Your mother and I, well, there's a temptation to hide things, try to pretend problems don't exist, or that you kids are unaware of what's going on. I see that's a mistake now. Maybe if we'd been more open, Michael ... In any event, family counseling is definitely in order, and your mother and I have vowed to each other to do everything we can to save our family."

"That's great, Dad," Jody said, but she felt uneasy. Why did it take Michael's being missing for two days for her parents to make those sorts of vows? And what if Michael took his own sweet time about getting back? Jody suddenly realized just how angry she was, and she turned away from her father. "I'm going to wait for Lauren outside," she said. "Okay?"

"Sure," her father said, glancing at the clock. Jody wondered if he was timing the minutes until Michael called, but knew better than to ask.

She sat under the oak tree out front and was pleased when she saw Lauren walking down her sidewalk. She got up immediately and ran over to Lauren. The two girls hugged, and Jody led her back to the shade of the tree.

"Did Michael run away?" Lauren asked. "Have you heard anything?"

"We hope he ran away," Jody replied. "Dad seems to think he did, at least this morning. There hasn't been any word. The police are sure he did, and that he'll call today, or come home on his own. School starts tomorrow, and they think he'll come to his senses, and come back here." She looked down at her fingernails and was surprised to see they were all bitten short. She'd given up biting her fingernails two years back.

"What do you think?" Lauren asked.

"I don't know what to think," Jody replied. "I was the last to see him and he was upset about things, but I don't think he was planning anything drastic. But if he didn't run away, then God only knows what could have happened to him, and we really don't want to think about those things. It's too scary. So I guess we'll figure he ran away and maybe he'll be in his own bed tonight."

"What can I do?" Lauren asked.

"Nothing," Jody replied. "Maybe you can talk to Kay. You know how she looks up to you, and she's hardly talking at all."

33

Lauren patted Jody's arm. "Michael will be back," she said. "I promise. He's not the kind of kid bad things happen to. He'll come back, and everything will return to normal, I promise."

Jody smiled ruefully. "Thanks, Lauren," she said. "But no matter what happens, nothing's going to be normal here again. We're going to have to learn to live with that, and when Michael gets back, so will he."

"It'll be okay," Lauren murmured, and Jody let herself pretend that was true. It didn't matter that Lauren had no idea what she was talking about. "It'll be okay" ran through her system like a gentle stream. "It'll be okay." After all, it had to be. What were the other choices?

Wednesday, September 4

*T*he school year began with the Pledge of Allegiance and a message on the loudspeaker about Michael.

"As some of you may have heard," the principal's disembodied voice proclaimed, "Michael Chapman, a member of this year's freshman class, has been missing since Sunday. Many of you have gone out searching through the woods for him, and I'm sure his family has appreciated all your efforts. I have not met Michael, but his sister Jody is a popular member of our junior class, and I know we're all eager to do whatever we can to help her and her family at this time."

Jody felt her face turn bright red. She had thought, foolishly, she realized now, that school would be a refuge from the situation at home, that at school at least, Michael would not be in her every thought, that she could concern herself, instead, with grades, and friendships, and even cheerleading.

But now any inhibitions that the kids might have had—the teachers too, for that matter—about asking her questions, besieging her with suggestions, swamping her with anecdotes about the time their sisters, their uncles, their dogs, disappeared, were gone, and Jody spent the day listening and nodding and answering. She should have known it would be bad, if she'd only let herself think about it, but she hadn't. There were enough bad things to think about as it was.

Maris and Lauren joined her for lunch, and they flanked her, and listened to all the kids who came up to Jody, wanting to share in her moment of celebrity. Jody let them take over the nodding and listening. She sat still for a moment, staring at the lunchroom line, realizing for the first time that Michael should have been there, that this was to have been his first day in high school, and the pain she felt was so intense she thought for sure everyone else in the room must have felt it also.

"I need some air," she whispered, and ran from the table, leaving her food, her books, and her friends behind. She left the cafeteria and walked outside, wanting to run away, to join Michael in his netherworld.

She stood resting against the front wall of the school building, hoping that no one would bother to rescue her, when she heard the sound of someone crying. Hidden behind some shrubs was Jerry Murphy, hiding his face in his hands, and sobbing.

Jody turned around quickly, not knowing what to do. It wasn't fair that she should have to share somebody else's pain, not then, not after a morning of being accosted by well-wishers and thrill-seekers. She stood absolutely still, closed her eyes, and willed Jerry to disappear, or at least to stop crying. But he continued to moan, and she licked her lips and walked over to him, kneeling by his side in the shrubbery.

"Jody," he said. "I'm sorry."

"It's okay," she said, willing herself not to cry. "First-day-of-school blues, huh?"

Jerry shook his head. "It's Michael," he said. "We said we were going to do everything together today, go to school and eat lunch, and walk home together and play ball. I didn't want you to see me cry. I didn't want anybody to. It's a baby thing."

"Then my father's a baby," Jody declared. "Because he's been crying on and off since Sunday. You think my father's a baby?"

"No," Jerry said.

"Neither do I," Jody said, sitting down next to him. "I miss

Michael an awful lot today, so I can understand why you would too."

"He's my best friend," Jerry said, sniffling.

Jody looked at Jerry and laughed. "You know how it is when someone throws up and you get sick to your stomach from the smell?" she asked.

Jerry nodded. "A couple of years ago, David Templeton threw up in gym, and half the kids were puking all around him," he said.

"Tears are the same way," Jody said. "Only not as smelly. I'll tell you what. I promise to try not to cry in front of you if you promise to try not to cry in front of me. We can cry all we want around other people, but when we're together, if one of us feels like crying, we'll say something silly instead."

"Like what?" Jerry asked.

"Oh, I don't know," Jody said. "Like 'David Templeton.' If one of us thinks we're going to start crying, then we say 'David Templeton,' and I bet we'll end up laughing instead. Is it a deal?"

"What if David Templeton is around when we say it?" Jerry asked, but Jody could see his tears were through, at least for the moment.

Jody grinned. "Then we'll both start crying," she said. "And poor David Templeton will have no idea why, and I bet he'll start crying too."

Jerry laughed. "David Templeton," he said. "It serves him right anyway, for throwing up and making us all sick in the gym. They had to spray with Lysol for weeks after he puked."

"David Templeton," Jody said. "It'll be our secret code, Jerry. Just yours and mine. We won't tell anybody else."

"Except Michael, when he gets back," Jerry said. "We can tell him, right?"

"Oh yeah," Jody said. "When Michael comes back, we'll let him in on our secret code."

"I feel better now," Jerry said. "Thanks, Jody."

"Thank *you*," she said, because the funny thing was, she felt better too.

Thursday, September 5

"I'm not going to school today," Kay announced at breakfast.

"What are you talking about?" her mother asked. "Of course you are. Now sit down and eat your breakfast."

"I am not!" Kay said. "And you can't make me."

"Shut up and eat your breakfast," her mother said. "You spoiled little brat."

"I am not spoiled," Kay said. "And I'm not going to school just because you say I have to. I hate school. I hate everything, and I'm not going."

"Kay," her father said.

Kay sat in her chair and folded her arms. "I'm not going to school and you can't make me," she declared. "You can't make me do anything I don't want to ever again."

"Eat your goddamned eggs and get ready for school," her mother whispered, fury burning in her eyes.

"Just try and make me," Kay said. "Because if you do, I'm just going to run away."

"Kay," Jody said, but it was too late. Her mother had already picked up her half-full coffee mug and flung it across the room. Coffee splattered on everything, including a few drops on Kay.

"Why did it have to be Michael!" her mother screamed at Kay, who sat there, her hands covering her face. "Why couldn't it have been you!"

They stood frozen for a moment, none of them even breathing, and then Kay began to sob and ran away from the table upstairs to her room.

Jody's mother began shaking, just her arms at first, and then the rest of her body, until she was contorted with shudders.

37

Jody's father sat absolutely still, and Jody could feel the tension in his body, his indecision about where to go, who needed him more, his wife or his daughter; and since he couldn't decide, he couldn't move. The look of anguish in his eyes made Jody gasp.

"I'll talk to Kay," she said, and forced herself to get up from her chair, walk out of the kitchen, away from her parents and toward her sister.

Kay's door was closed, but Jody could hear her angry cries from the other end of the hallway. She opened the door without asking permission, and walked over to Kay's bed. "Stop it," she said. "Stop crying. You hear me?"

Kay continued to sob.

Jody thought of David Templeton and resisted the temptation to start laughing. She bit hard on her lip, took a deep breath and said, "You're acting like a baby, and you promised you wouldn't."

"I am not acting like a baby!" Kay screamed, and she turned her body toward Jody's and began swinging at her, pounding at her with her fists. The fury in Kay's eyes was matched by the strength of her punches, and Jody, who was determined not to resist, to let Kay work some of her pain out on her, was forced to duck away before her own anger took over.

"All right," she said, pushing Kay's arms away from her. "All right, Kay. I'm sorry."

"I am not a baby!" Kay shouted, but then she collapsed on the bed and looked for all the world as though she was about to suck her thumb.

Jody sat on the bed next to her. Her shoulders and chest hurt from Kay's punches.

Kay looked up at her sister. "Mom had no right to say that," she said. "She had no right."

"I agree," Jody said. "But you had to know it would drive her crazy when you threatened to run away."

"She never listens to me," Kay said. "She never did before anyway, but now it's even worse. Last night, all I wanted to do was tell her how awful school was, how all the teachers came up to me asking me about Michael, where he was, what was happening. It was my first day at school without Michael being there.

Last year, when I started middle school, everyone knew Michael, and no one knew me, and I was just Michael Chapman's kid sister, but yesterday, it was all supposed to be different. Yesterday, I was going to be in middle school, and Michael would be starting high school, and he'd just be your kid brother, and I'd be the important one. But Michael might as well have been there with me. Nobody cared about me yesterday. Nobody's cared about me since Michael disappeared. All they ever talk about is Michael, and you sometimes. They say, 'Isn't Jody wonderful, the way she's holding up. Jody's just a pillar of strength.' That's what Daddy called you yesterday. A pillar of strength. And me, they tell me not to act like a baby, and I'm not acting like a baby, and then Mom hugs me until I think I'm going to suffocate and she says, 'If anything ever happened to you, I think I'd die,' and I can't breathe and I hate everyone and I especially hate Michael because it's all his fault. And she had no right to throw that mug at me, and she had no right to say she wished it was me and not him."

"I know," Jody said. "But you provoked her and she lost control. She didn't mean to hurt you."

"Of course she did," Kay said. "And Daddy didn't do anything to stop her. Doesn't he care about me?"

"Not now," Jody replied. "He doesn't care these days. None of us do. Dad cares about himself, and Mom cares about herself, and I care about me. We don't care about each other. But neither do you."

"I do too," Kay protested.

"No, you don't," Jody replied. "If you did, you wouldn't have said you weren't going to school today, and you certainly wouldn't have made that crack about running away. We're all locked up right now in our own pain, and none of us is thinking very much about anybody else, except maybe Michael."

"I think about him all the time," Kay said. "I think he's dead, but I don't dare tell anybody. I dream he's dead too, but only I know, and when I try to tell Mom and Dad the words just won't come out."

"I dream he's locked up somewhere," Jody said. "And I keep reaching for the key to free him, but it shifts away from me and I can never get to it. He's crying and I'm crying, and the key keeps moving."

"Do you think Mom and Dad are having dreams like that?" Kay asked.

"When they can sleep," Jody said. "Neither one of them really has in the past few days."

"I don't want to go to school," Kay said.

"I know," Jody said. "I don't want to go to school either. But I think we have to."

"Why?" Kay asked, but at least she was sitting up.

"A lot of reasons," Jody replied. "Mom and Dad want us to, for starters, and they have enough on their minds without us making things worse by not doing what they want. And if we don't go to school today, then when we do go back tomorrow, everybody's going to wonder why we cut today, and we'll have to answer a thousand questions, and tomorrow will turn out to be as bad as yesterday was."

"Couldn't we just not go to school until Michael gets back?" Kay asked. "Mom and Dad aren't going to work."

"They will on Monday, I think," Jody said. "Of course, Michael should be back before then, but if he isn't, I know Dad is planning on going back."

"Is he dead?" Kay asked. "You're the only person I can ask that, Jody."

"I don't think so," Jody said. "I really don't. If he was dead, then I think they'd have found something by now."

"You mean like his body?" Kay said.

"Yeah," Jody said. "I guess that *is* what I mean. And they haven't found anything that looks like he might be dead, so I don't think he is."

"What if he never comes back?" Kay asked. "What if we spend the rest of our lives waiting and waiting and he never comes back?"

Jody sighed. "I don't know what happens then," she said. "I suppose we just get along with our lives, go to school, do our homework, eat supper, talk to our friends. We just keep on living and waiting."

"And crying," Kay said.

40

"And crying," Jody said. "You ready to go to school now?"

"No," Kay replied. "But I guess I have to."

Jody nodded. "Come on," she said. "I'll walk you to school, and then I'll go on to the high school."

"You'll be late," Kay said.

Jody shrugged. "They'll forgive me," she said.

Kay embraced Jody, and Jody flinched from the pain. She'd be bruised for days, she realized. That was her last episode as a voluntary punching bag.

"I don't want to see Mommy," Kay said. "She'll cry and say she's sorry and I don't want her to right now."

"All right," Jody said. "You finish getting ready for school, and I'll go downstairs and tell Mom we're leaving through the front door. She'll understand."

"I don't care if she does," Kay said. "She doesn't understand me. Not the way you do, Jody. Nobody understands me the way you do."

"Yeah," Jody said, feeling the bruises that proved it. "Come on, Kay. Let's get out of here. No matter what, school's bound to be better than this."

Friday, September 6

"Jody, I'm worried about you," Lauren said as they set their lunch trays down at their table.

"Worried?" Jody said. "For heaven's sake, why?"

"It's what you've been eating lately," Lauren said. "Look at this tray. You have a package of cheese crackers with peanut butter, a slice of apple pie, a piece of chocolate cake, and a cup of fruit punch. That's your lunch?"

"It's all I feel like eating," Jody said.

"I bet you haven't been eating sensibly at home either,"

Lauren said. "When was the last time your mother made a normal dinner?"

"We don't eat normal dinners anymore," Jody said. "But we have takeout a lot. Pizza, and Chinese. Last night, we had . . ." She paused for a moment, trying to remember. "Well, I don't know what we had, but it was real food."

"What's this about real food?" Maris asked, joining them at the table. Jody grinned at her.

"Lauren's worried about my lunches," Jody said.

"I don't blame her," Maris declared. "Look at that junk. You'll end up looking like a blimp if you don't watch it, Jody."

"It isn't the weight I'm worried about," Lauren said. "It's what that kind of diet does to your system. You have to keep your strength up, and all that sugar is just going to zap it away from you."

"I'll start eating more sensibly later," Jody said. When Michael comes home, she thought to herself, the way she always did now. I'll concentrate on my schoolwork when Michael comes home. I'll straighten out my room when Michael comes home. I'll eat more sensibly, brush my teeth more regularly, jog every day, watch less TV, stop biting my nails, my lips, my tongue, when Michael comes home. I'll start sleeping again, and breathing again, and laughing again, when Michael comes home. I'll be Jody Chapman again when Michael comes home. I'll be alive again when Michael comes home.

"Diet is very important," Lauren said. "You can't underestimate how important diet is."

"Don't talk to me about diets," Maris said. "My mother's on one, so she can fit into all those bikinis she bought last week. Starvation diet. Two glasses of water in the morning, two at lunch, two for supper, and one for a midnight snack. The only solid food she's allowed are saltines, so she'll be thirsty and drink even more water."

"Saltines and water are just as bad as cake and pie," Lauren said. "I'm glad to see you're eating a sensible meal, Maris."

"I have to," Maris said cheerfully. "This is it for me. Mom won't let me eat in front of her while she's on this diet, so there's nothing in the house except saltines. And I can't eat too many of them, because Mom counts them every day to make sure she's only eaten the half dozen she's allowed. So lunch here is what I get to eat nowadays. It used to be when Mom would go on one of these crazy diets, I'd just have supper every night at the Chapmans'. But they aren't eating all that much better right now, are you, Jody?"

"We eat takeout," Jody replied. "I guess it's balanced enough."

"Your mother is such a good cook too," Maris said. "I can't wait until things get back to normal with your family, so I can start eating there again."

"We're looking forward to it too," Jody said. Another thing to add to the When Michael Comes Home list.

"I'm going back on that line and get you something healthy to eat," Lauren announced. "A tuna salad sandwich. Milk. Anything else you'd like, Jody? Maybe some fruit?"

"Don't bother," Jody said. "The pie is full of fruit, and the cake has milk in it, and the peanut butter is practically pure protein, and the fruit punch is vitamin-enriched. What I have here is just as good for me as a regular lunch, and this I'll eat."

Lauren sat back in her chair. "You have to eat sensibly to maintain your strength," she declared. "It's very important that you stay strong for your family."

"I know," Jody said.

"I wish I could check up on you," Lauren replied. "Maybe I'll call later."

"No, don't do that," Jody said. "We don't like it when the phone rings. We always think it has to do with Michael."

"She won't let me call either," Maris said to Lauren. "It's driving me crazy. It used to be when Mom was in an ugly drunk, I'd go over to Jody's, or at least lock myself in the bathroom and take the phone with me, and call Jody and talk to her until Mom calmed down or passed out. But now I can't go over there, and I can't call her up, and I'm stuck in the bathroom, with Mom pounding on the door shouting that I'm no damn good. It's been awful."

"I don't understand you at all, Maris," Lauren declared,

putting her fork down on her plate with a loud clatter. "How can you go on about your problems when Jody is in such pain?"

"Jody isn't the only one in pain," Maris replied. "She knows that."

"But what do you know?" Lauren asked. "When was the last time you asked Jody anything about Michael?"

"I don't have to ask," Maris replied. "There's no news. Jody would tell me if they'd heard anything."

"If you ever closed your mouth long enough to listen," Lauren said. "Jody, I want to apologize for Maris. She's so involved in her own petty little problems, she's lost all sight of what's really important."

"You don't have to apologize for me, Lauren Clark," Maris said. "Nobody has to apologize for me. Do they, Jody?"

"Don't pay any attention to her, Jody," Lauren said. "Maris simply thinks the world revolves around her and her no-good mother."

"Don't you call my mother no good!" Maris shouted. "My mother is every bit as good as yours. And I hate the way you act like you're the only one who knows what's good for Jody. 'Poor little Jody' this and 'poor little Jody' that. Like you love her more than I do somehow, or better. That's just a lot of crap."

"At least I'm sensitive toward her feelings," Lauren said. "Which is a lot more than you've been."

"Jody, tell Lauren she's full of crap," Maris demanded.

"What?" Jody said.

The girls stared at her. "Jody, haven't you been listening at all?" Maris asked.

Jody shook her head. "I was thinking about Michael," she said. "Wondering if Michael is locked up somewhere, or if he's free, able to move around if he wants. What do you think? Do either of you have any ideas where Michael could be?"

Sunday, September 8

*A*t a quarter to one that afternoon, Jody made herself comfortable on the window seat in the living room. She had her English textbook by her side, for decorative effect, and Baron curled up next to her for comfort. It had been a week since Jody had seen Michael, exactly a week since he was on his way to Jerry's house. David Templeton, she thought automatically. Lately she couldn't think of Jerry without David Templeton's name popping into her mind, like a hiccup.

A week before things had been normal, or at least what was passing for normal. A week ago, she had fingernails and daydreams and perfectly average concerns. A week ago she had been a hundred years younger.

But now a week had passed and there had been no word from Michael, no sight of him, no knowledge of where he was, how he was. The past week had been nothing but pain and fear and horror, and now that week was ending, and Michael would be coming back.

Jody wasn't sure when she knew Michael would be returning that afternoon, as close to one o'clock as he could make it, but when she woke up that morning—at five was it? or a quarter after?—she had known. She hadn't told anyone, because there was no point getting everyone else's hopes up, but she'd known. It would be a *Twilight Zone* kind of a thing, where Michael had simply stepped into another dimension by mistake, made a left into infinity when he should have walked straight ahead, and after a week he'd have gotten his sense of direction back and would know the way home, the way back to reality. Jody had realized that at five that morning, and she never lost her sense of sureness that at one o'clock that afternoon Michael would walk back in, back to his own personal universe.

Jody didn't care what stories Michael would have to tell; they were unimportant. The papers would want to know where he'd been, and the police, and her parents, but all that mattered for her was his safe return. She would never tease him again. When Michael Comes Home, I will be a better sister.

"What're you doing?"

"Kay!" Jody said. "Kay, go away."

"Why?" Kay asked. "What're you doing?"

"Nothing," Jody said. "Kay, just leave me alone for a while, all right? I'll explain it all later." Later, when no explanations would be needed.

"You're waiting for Michael," Kay said. "Why can't I wait with you?"

"I don't know," Jody said. "But you can't. You weren't here a week ago when he disappeared, so you can't be here now."

"Everything's different from a week ago," Kay pointed out. "Dad and Mom are both here, and they were out then too. Michael was here, and now he's gone. And I bet you weren't curled up on the window seat with your English book a week ago either. So why can't I keep you company while you wait?"

"Because you can't," Jody said. "Go talk with Mom and Dad."

"I'd rather die," Kay said. "I'll just sit in the corner over there and wait with you. I won't say anything."

"Kay," Jody snarled, but it didn't matter. Kay curled up on the corner chair and stared out the window with Jody.

"There you are," their father said, walking into the living room. "We were wondering where you'd both gone to."

"We're here doing our homework," Jody said, grabbing her textbook for display. "That's all we're up to."

"Mind if I join you?" her father asked. "I'll just sit here and work on the crossword puzzle. I won't disturb you."

"All right," Jody said with a sigh. Kay giggled from her corner, and Jody scowled. It doesn't matter, she told herself. The time is right for Michael to come home, and the United States Marines could be waiting in the living room for him, and he'd show up. She flipped through her textbook until she found the weekend's assigned reading, and tried to concentrate on it.

"Why are you all in the living room?" her mother asked, walking in, rubbing her hands. She'd been doing that all week, Jody realized. Rubbing her hands, to get some blood into them.

"I don't know," Jody's father replied. "We just seem to have wandered in here."

"I think I'll join you then," Jody's mother said. "I've been meaning to get back to my knitting." She got out her bag of yarn, and soon the silence was punctuated by the clicking noises of needles hitting against each other.

They sat that way for over an hour, none of them saying a word, involved in their own projects, only looking up, frequently at first, and then at longer and longer intervals, at the window, toward the door, waiting for the week to end, waiting for Michael to return. And when by two o'clock there was no Michael, one by one they left the room, Kay to her bedroom, her mother to the kitchen, her father to the backyard, which he began to mow, and only Jody remained at the window seat, staring out, listening to the sound of the mower, as her hopes for Michael died one by one.

CELEBRATIONS

Thursday, September 12

"Jody, I need to talk to you."

"Sure, Kay," Jody said, letting Kay into her bedroom. "What's up?"

"This may sound dumb," Kay said. "But what are you doing about Michael's birthday?"

"Birthday?" Jody said.

"His birthday's on Saturday," Kay said. "Are you buying him anything?"

"Michael's gone," Jody said. "He's been gone for almost two weeks."

"I know that," Kay declared. "Everybody knows that. But what if he comes home on Saturday, for his birthday? You know what a big fuss Michael likes for his birthdays. Mom has to get just the right kind of cake, and every year he wants to have a bigger and bigger party, and he always expects great presents. If he comes back Saturday, and we don't have a party ready for him, and all the presents he wants, then maybe he'll run away again."

"We don't know that he ran away," Jody said, running her fingers through her hair.

"Have you bought him anything?" Kay asked.

"Of course not," Jody said. "I don't buy presents for people who aren't here. When Michael gets back, then I'll go out and get him something. But not until then. I'm not spending a single cent of my own money on a present for somebody who just disappears."

"But you said he might not have run away," Kay said. "If he didn't run away, then it isn't his fault he isn't here for his birthday, so why shouldn't you buy him a present?"

"Kay, if you want to buy Michael a present, then buy him

51

something," Jody said. "Just leave me out of it. I have better things to do with my money."

"Like what?" Kay asked.

"I don't know," Jody said. "But anything's got to be better than buying a present for somebody who's been away for almost two weeks. My own birthday's coming up too, you know, and yours also. Maybe I'm saving up my money to get myself something really great. Or something for you. What would you like for your birthday this year?"

"I'd like Michael to come back," Kay replied.

"Fine," Jody said. "You can wish for that when you blow out the candles. I'll wish for world peace. We both have the same chance of getting what we want."

"What's with you?" Kay asked. "You're the one who's always saying he's coming back."

"I don't want him coming back if he's just dropping in to pick up his presents," Jody declared. "I don't need a brother like that. If Michael wants a birthday celebration, then let him earn it by making his bed and doing his homework."

"You're crazy," Kay said. "You've finally gone crazy."

"Maybe I have," Jody replied. "But Kay, I miss him so much. And the thought that he's going to turn fourteen away from us, God only knows where, right now, I'd just rather hate him."

"I didn't know it was okay to hate him," Kay said. "I thought we just had to miss him and love him and worry about him all the time."

"We do," Jody said. "Miss him and love him and worry about him and hate him. Until he comes home."

"Then I guess I won't buy him anything," Kay said. "I'll save the money, so when he comes home, I'll be able to buy him something. I wonder what he'll want then, what he'll be like."

"He'll be like Michael," Jody replied. "And he'll want something big and expensive, the way he always does."

"I'll save up my money for it," Kay said. "And when he comes home, I'll buy him the biggest, most expensive thing I can find."

"Fair enough," Jody said. "And Kay?"

"Yeah?"

"Try not to hate him," Jody said. "Wherever he is, I bet he's missing us as much as we miss him."

"I know," Kay said. "Wanna bet he shows up Saturday? It would be just like him."

"No bets," Jody said. "Just prayers."

Saturday, September 14

"Well, isn't anyone going to eat this cake?" Jody's mother demanded, as they sat around the kitchen table after dinner that night.

"Linda, it's a birthday cake," Jody's father said. "It even says 'Happy Birthday Michael' on it."

"Of course it's a birthday cake," her mother replied. "It's Michael's favorite kind too. Chocolate layers, with butter cream. And blue roses. Michael always says pink roses are for girls, but he loves to eat them, so I got them made in blue. We'll save a piece with roses for him. Come on, who wants the first piece?"

"No thanks, Mom," Jody said. "I'm really not hungry."

"Do you think we should sing 'Happy Birthday' first?" Jody's mother asked. "No candles, because Michael should be here to blow them out, but there's no reason why we can't sing 'Happy Birthday.' He'd want us to. I bet he'll hear us, wherever he is, if we sing it loudly enough."

"Linda," Jody's father said, and he touched his wife gently on her arm.

"No, Tom, this is important," Jody's mother said. "Come on, Kay. Let's sing 'Happy Birthday' so loud it would wake up the dead. I mean . . ." And she stood there, knife poised in her hand, and began to cry over the cake.

Jody's father moved her away from the table, and embraced her. Kay began to cry as well. Jody stared at all of them and thought about smashing the cake, demolishing each and every one of the blue roses, but she closed her eyes instead and did nothing.

The phone rang, and Jody, glad for a chance to do something, ran to answer it. "Hello?" she said, and in spite of herself she felt sure it would be Michael.

"This is Jack Dino," the voice said.

"Officer Dino," Jody said. "Hi. Have you heard anything?"

"No," he said. "I was calling to see if you had."

"Nothing," Jody said. "Do you want to talk to my father?"

"No, that isn't necessary," Officer Dino replied. "Damn. I was sure Michael would be back in touch with you by his birthday."

"We haven't heard a thing," Jody told him. She felt an urge to invite him over for birthday cake, but kept the thought to herself. "We were just talking about it, about how today is his birthday, and we haven't heard anything."

"Look, it doesn't mean anything," Officer Dino said, clearing his throat. "Lots of runaways, it takes them a while to come to their senses, realize that home is the best place for them. More than two weeks. A month maybe, maybe even more."

"You don't still think he ran away, do you?" Jody asked.

"I don't know," Dino admitted. "I pray he did though."

"Don't waste your prayers," Jody said. "Good-bye, Officer." She hung up the phone and looked around. The others were staring at her.

"Any word?" her mother asked.

"Of course not," Jody said. "He wouldn't have talked to me if he had anything important to say. Mom, if we skip the singing, I'll eat a piece of that cake now."

"Me too," Kay said. "A big piece with lots of flowers."

"We really should sing," their mother said, but she cut a slice, and then another, and another, until the cake was cut into a dozen pieces, and they all grabbed pieces with their fingers, and ate the sugary sweetness that was Michael's favorite.

Wednesday, October 2

"Oh, no!" Jody's mother cried as she looked at the calendar.

"What is it?" her father asked, finishing his second cup of coffee.

"Sunday is Jody's birthday," her mother said. "Her sixteenth birthday, and we haven't done anything about it."

"It's okay, Mom," Jody said, washing down her toast with some orange juice. "We've had other things on our minds."

"But we have to do something for your sixteenth birthday," her mother declared. "It's so special. I guess we don't have enough time to plan for a big party, but we should have some kind of a celebration. We just have to."

"Mom, none of us are exactly in a celebrating mood these days," Jody said. "I'm willing to skip it this year, so don't worry about it."

"But it isn't fair," her mother said. "And Kay's birthday is in a couple of weeks too. How could I have let things slide like this?"

"Linda, don't make such a big fuss about it," her husband said. "The girls understand, don't you?"

"Sure, Dad," Jody said, and stared at her sister.

"I'd like a party," Kay said. "I've been scared to ask. Can I have a party this year, Mom?"

"Of course you can," her mother said. "And so can Jody. We'll just call everybody tonight and see if they're free this weekend. Would you rather have something Saturday night or Sunday afternoon?"

"I don't want a party, Mom," Jody said. "Not the way things are now. Next year we'll have a big party instead."

"We can't keep putting things off," her mother declared. "That's how we got into this mess in the first place. I was going to write out invitations for your birthday party on Labor Day, I remember, I had it all planned, and if I'd just stuck with my plan, we wouldn't have to make all these last-minute phone calls. Sunday afternoon would probably be better. Your friends might already have dates for Saturday night. We'll have a Sunday afternoon football party. How does that sound, Jody? A touch football game, hot dogs, popcorn. And cake, of course."

"Don't bother, Mom," Jody said. "Besides, my friends would all think it was weird."

"Weird?" her mother said. "What's weird about celebrating a birthday?"

Jody remembered the way they'd killed Michael's birthday cake and tried not to laugh. "They just would, that's all," she said. "Let's skip the party this year, all right? Next year, I promise, we can have a big party."

"I have an idea," Jody's father said. "How about if the four of us go to church together Sunday morning, and then go out for brunch afterwards? We haven't been together in church as a family in a long time, and we could celebrate Jody's birthday that way. Then we could have cake and presents after we got home from brunch."

"I'm not going to church," Kay declared. "I'm not going to pray to any dumb God that takes my brother away from me."

"God did not take Michael away," her father said.

"Well, He sure hasn't brought him back," Kay said. "I prayed every single night all last month that Michael would come back, that he was okay and he'd come back, and he never did. I'm through with praying and I'm through with church, and I'm not going back as long as Michael's gone."

"Going to church has nothing to do with Michael," her father said. "If I say you're going to church, then you're going to church. Do you hear me, young lady?"

"I'm not going," Kay said.

"I'm not going either," her mother said.

"Linda!" Jody's father said.

"I agree with Kay," her mother said. "I've prayed too, and everybody I know has prayed, and God hasn't heard any of our prayers and I give up."

"You don't just give up on God," Jody's father said. "If you give up on Him, then He might just give up on you."

"And you don't think He has?" Jody's mother cried. "You honestly think a caring God would put us through all this? Kay is right. Church is no place for us right now. You can go with Jody if you want, but I'm staying home."

"You can't stay home," Jody's father said. "What will people think?"

"I know exactly what they're thinking," Jody's mother said. "They're thinking we're monsters, forcing our son to run away. They think we're the worst kind of parents, unable to keep our family together. They think Michael is dead, and they don't know what to say to us, so they cough and turn away and act as though we're dead too. I don't need that in church. I get it at work, and at the supermarket, and in the parking lot. Those looks of pity and disgust. There's fear in their eyes too, because they know what happened to Michael can happen to any one of their children as well, and they avoid me, and try to pretend that they don't. I hate them. I hate all of them, and I hate you too, Tom. This never would have happened if you hadn't gone away that weekend. If you'd just stayed home, talked things out with me instead of insisting on going away 'to think,' then Michael would still be here. This is all your fault, and it's about time somebody said it, because you're to blame, you and that God you say we should make nice with. It's all your fault, and I hate you."

"Linda," her husband said.

"No," she said. "It's true, and you know it. We all know it, we've just been afraid to admit it. Girls, get ready for school. You don't have much time left."

"Mom, we can't just go to school now," Jody said. "You can't say things like that and then just expect us to pack our books and go off to school."

"Then stay. See if I care," her mother said. "I'm leaving."

"Where are you going to?" her husband asked.

"What do you care?" she replied. "I'm going out. I'll be back, don't worry. I'm not going to leave you until Michael gets back, and then I'm taking the kids, and you'll never see any of us again."

"Linda, you have to go to work," her husband said. "You can't just storm off like this."

"I gave them my notice on Monday," she declared. "So they

can fire me if they want for being irresponsible, and it won't make any difference."

"Mom, you can't leave," Kay pleaded. "Mom, I can't lose you too. I'll go to church. I'll keep my room clean. I'll do anything you say, but don't leave us."

"What makes you think I care?" her mother said, and stormed out. The dishes on the table shook from the vibrations of the door.

"She'll be back," Jody said to Kay. "She's just mad right now."

"I don't care if she never comes back," Kay said. "Dad can disappear too for all I care. I'm going to school now, just the way she wants me to. No matter how bad things are at school, they're better than they are here. I hate all of you. You're all crazy and I hate you all, and I wish you'd all just leave me alone and die." She got up from the table and ran upstairs.

Jody began clearing off the table. "You'd better get a move on, Dad," she said. "Or you'll be late for work."

"So I'm late," he said. "So what difference does that make?"

"It makes a big difference," Jody said. "If Mom's quit her job, then you'd better keep yours."

"I guess," he said. "Jody, what did I do wrong?"

"You mean today?" Jody asked. "Or with Michael?"

"Today," he said. "Just now. I know everything I did wrong with Michael. What went wrong today?"

"Nothing that I can see," Jody said, loading the dishes into the dishwasher. "You said we should go to church on my birthday. That's all. It sounded reasonable enough to me. At least as good as a football party."

"Michael is my only son," Jody's father declared. "I don't think it's so strange that I should want to pray for his safe return."

"It isn't strange," Jody said. "Come on, Dad, go to work."

"We were never a completely happy family," Jody's father said. "There have always been problems. Linda needs so much, I can't always give her what she needs, and I resent it sometimes, how demanding she is, how one-sided it can be. But this. This is so unfair, Jody, so uncalled-for. I'm not a bad man, and your mother is not a bad woman. God really screwed up this time."

"I think we all did, Dad," Jody said, wiping the table off with a sponge. "God might have started us off this way, but ever since then, we've been messing up just fine on our own."

Sunday, October 6

Jody woke up early on her birthday and realized how very little she wanted to deal with anyone in her family. She felt a brief moment of shame, but then she thought about how crazy they all were, and how just breathing on a birthday automatically meant shouting and pain, and she chucked her guilt right out the window. She got dressed, used the downstairs bathroom to cut down the chances of waking anyone, warmed up some leftover Danish, and left the house by a quarter after seven, not sure what she was going to do with the day, but knowing she was going to spend it sanely somehow.

She'd walked a block away from home when she realized how upset her parents would be to find she was missing. Jody felt angry, and then she sighed. It used to be she'd leave all the time without bothering to tell anyone, or at least so it felt, now that she was no longer able to. But these days even a trip to the bathroom had to be announced, and an unexplained walk could result in mass hysteria. So she walked back home, opened the kitchen door, and stared at the kitchen table, trying to think what message would be acceptable for her family, without encouraging them to join her.

"Need some time alone," she finally wrote on the scrap pad her mother kept by the telephone. "See you after church." Until she wrote it, Jody hadn't realized she wanted to go to church, but seeing it down on paper like that made it seem like a good idea. Her family had gone to church the week after Michael's disappearance, and again the week after that, but the past couple

59

of weeks they'd slept in on Sunday. Church seemed like a refuge, and a refuge was exactly what Jody was in the mood for.

Services weren't for another hour and a half though, so Jody used the time to walk around town. The posters about Michael were still up, but she was used to them by now. It no longer startled her to see her brother's face staring out from storefronts and on telephone poles. When the posters had first gone up, each time Jody had unexpectedly seen one, she'd gotten confused, and thought that it really was Michael, or at least some evidence as to where he was. But now they were just part of the landscape, along with the chrysanthemums and marigolds.

Jody felt an urge to tear one of the Michael posters down, to shred it into a thousand little pieces, turn it into confetti in celebration of her birthday, but she walked away fast before she gave in to the temptation. If she took one down, then other people might too, and then there might be no posters left of Michael, and just maybe it would be a poster that would jog somebody's memory and reveal to them what had become of him. The posters had to stay up. Celebrations would have to come from different sources.

She sat for a long time by Drake Pond, and then got up and walked to church. It felt strange going in without her parents, but by then everything in her life felt strange, so that was okay. Jody wondered how it would be when things ceased feeling strange, and whether she would like that any better.

The church service at least felt fairly normal, and Jody enjoyed the protective shield her family problem had created. Nobody asked her where her parents or Kay were. They probably thought the whole family had disappeared, leaving only her behind, Jody thought with a smile. Of course, for all she knew, they had. Jody had given up assuming people were where they should be unless she could see them with her own eyes.

Jody sang the hymns, said the prayers, listened to the sermon, and felt, if not at peace, then at least a little less at war than she had for a month. It felt wonderful not to be with her family, the best birthday present she could have given herself.

When the service ended Jody slipped out as inconspicuously as she could. The minister would be bound to ask about her family if she gave him any opportunity to, and she wasn't in the mood to answer his solicitous questions. Feeling like a spy, she wormed her way out of the crowd, and was halfway down the sidewalk before she became aware of two bodies pressing against her.

"This is a hijacking," Maris declared. "You have no choice but to come with us."

"Happy birthday," Lauren said. "Of course you have a choice, but we're hoping you won't exercise it."

"She does not have a choice," Maris said. "Jody Chapman, you are our prisoner."

Jody giggled. "Where are you taking me, warden?" she asked.

"To my house," Lauren said. "It's okay. Your mother knows."

"And how long's my sentence?"

"Until three this afternoon," Lauren said. "With time off for good behavior."

"No early release, please," Jody said. "Let me serve my full time."

"See, I told you," Maris crowed. "Jody, Lauren thought maybe you wouldn't want anybody to make a fuss over your birthday because of Michael and everything, but I said of course you would, one thing has absolutely nothing to do with the other, and I was right. As always."

"I do have one favor to ask of you," Jody said. "And then I promise to be a well-behaved prisoner. Please don't mention Michael again today."

"Fair enough," Lauren said. "Come on, Jody, your celebration awaits."

The girls jogged the rest of the way to Lauren's house. It was a beautiful autumn day and Jody loved the sensation of being guarded by her two closest friends. Lauren opened the front door, and Jody was accosted by the sound of "SURPRISE!" being shouted at her from the living room.

Sure enough, a dozen of her friends were in the room, wearing party hats and looking generally foolish. Jody thought she'd burst into tears, decided she'd better not, and grinned instead.

"I don't believe this," she said. "You organized a party. How did you manage that?"

"Skill and planning," Maris said. "Happy birthday, Jody."

"Thank you," Jody said. "Thanks, all of you."

"It wasn't anything," Jim Adams said. "I never turn down party invitations."

"Come on, Jody, Mom's making pancakes and waffles," Lauren declared. "And then we're going to play volleyball and touch football, and then we'll have lunch and birthday cake."

"There might even be some birthday presents," Maris said. "My mother bought you a box of saltines."

Jody laughed. "Bring on the pancakes," she said. "Or do I want waffles?"

"You want both," Ginny Morrisey declared. "At least I want both, and I refuse to pig out unless you do."

"Come and get them!" Lauren's mother called out from the kitchen, and Jody and her friends all stormed in there. The plates and the syrups and honey were all awaiting them, and there was a lot of noise and motion as the kids served themselves.

Jody stood still for a moment and looked at her friends. She caught Maris's eye, and Maris winked at her. Jody winked back. For one glorious moment, she was almost happy again.

Tuesday, October 8

"It was lovely of Maris and Lauren to plan a party for you," Jody's mother declared as they sat around the kitchen table after supper. "But we're not going to have any slipups with Kay's. Tomorrow I'll call her friends, and invite them myself. You're satisfied with your list, Kay? You have until tomorrow to add other names to it."

"It's fine, Mom," Kay replied. "I don't want lots of people. Just my real close friends."

"If you change your mind, let me know," her mother said. "Jody, you'll help me with the party plans, won't you? I want some festivity in this house, crepe paper, and streamers. Twelve is a very important age, you know. As important as sixteen."

"I'll be happy to help," Jody said. "Any color scheme you want, Kay?"

Kay shook her head. "It doesn't have to be too fancy," she declared. "You'll come, won't you, Jody?"

"I wouldn't miss it," Jody replied. "You sure you don't want more than six kids?"

"Positive," Kay said. "The kids have been acting kind of weird lately. You know."

"Sure," Jody said. She and Kay had developed a shorthand language all their own. "Kind of weird" meant Kay's friends had been avoiding her, not knowing what to say, and therefore trying to get away without saying anything. Jody glanced at her parents, wondering if they had any understanding of what school was like for Kay, and, to a lesser extent, herself. If they did, they weren't showing it. Jody's mother was making a list, and her father was reading the newspaper.

"We won't need a large cake if it's less than a dozen people," Jody's mother said. "Do you still like lemon cream filling the best, Kay?"

Kay nodded. "With pink roses," she said.

"Pink roses are the best," her mother agreed. "If the weather is warm enough, maybe we'll have an end-of-season barbecue. Would you like that?"

"Sure," Kay said. "Whatever you want, Mom."

"It's your party, Kay," her mother replied. "If you don't want a barbecue, say so now."

"A barbecue would be great," Kay said, exchanging looks with Jody.

"I'm glad I'm not working anymore," Jody's mother declared. "It gives me so much more time to make arrangements for parties."

"Life is one constant party, all right," Jody's father said from behind the newspaper.

"If I hadn't been working, Michael would still be here," Jody's mother said. "And I, for one, intend to learn from my mistakes."

Jody's father grunted from behind his newspaper.

"A barbecue sounds great, Mom," Kay said. "Do you think you'll make your own barbecue sauce?"

"Of course I will," her mother said. "For a special occasion like your twelfth birthday, you'd better believe it. Would you like me to make some ice cream too? I haven't done that in a while."

"That would be great," Kay said. "It sounds like a wonderful party, Mom. Thank you."

"You have nothing to thank me for," her mother said. "Saturday the nineteenth at one o'clock. Six of your friends and four of us. Five, if Michael's back by then."

"Right," Kay said. "Barbecue and cake and ice cream. It sounds like the perfect party."

Saturday, October 19

"The house looks wonderful!" Kay declared. "Thank you, Jody. I love the crepe paper. And the balloons are terrific. Where did you find any that said 'Happy Birthday, Kay'?"

"It wasn't easy," Jody admitted. "But for you it was worth the search. Happy birthday, kid." She gave her sister a kiss on the forehead.

"And doesn't the barbecue smell great?" Kay continued. "I'm so hungry. I hope everybody comes right away, so we can start eating before it rains."

"It might not rain," Jody said. "It is your birthday, after all."

"It'll rain," Kay replied. "But I don't care. And Jody, thank you for my birthday present. How did you know I've been wanting a nightshirt?"

"Because that was what I wanted when I turned twelve," Jody declared. "No more baby pajamas."

"I'll wear it the next time I'm invited to a sleepover," Kay said. "Maybe after this party, kids won't be so scared to invite me places anymore."

"I sure hope so," Jody said. "I'm going to the kitchen now to see if Mom needs any help. You can open the door yourself when your friends arrive, can't you, Kay?"

"I think I can manage," Kay replied, and gave her sister another hug. "Thanks, Jody," she said. "For everything."

"Any time," Jody said, checking her watch as she left. It was already ten after one, and nobody had shown up yet. "You did tell everyone one o'clock," she whispered to her mother, as she entered the kitchen.

"Of course I did," her mother replied. "It's not that late. They'll probably all show up in the next five minutes."

But five minutes passed, and then another five, and still nobody came. Jody went back into the living room first to wait with Kay, and then her mother joined them.

"I'll start calling," her mother said. "Maybe I said two by mistake."

"You said one," Kay replied. "I was there."

"Then maybe they heard two," her mother said. "I'll wait until one-thirty, and if nobody's come by then, I'll call."

So they waited the five minutes staring at the front door, and still nobody showed.

"I'll start calling," Jody's mother said.

"No," Kay said. "Don't call. Please."

"Don't be silly," her mother said, but as she walked over to the phone, it rang on its own. "See?" her mother said, picking it up. "Hello? Oh hello, Margaret. Yes, yes, I see. Well, I'm terribly sorry, but of course I understand. I hope she feels better tomorrow." And she hung up.

"Julie isn't coming," Kay said.

"She has the flu," her mother said. "One of those twenty-four-hour things."

"Sure," Kay said. "That's what they all have."

"At least Margaret had the courtesy to call," her mother said, tapping the phone with her fingers. "What do you think? Should I call the others, or should we wait for them to call us?"

"It doesn't matter," Kay said. "Nobody's going to come."

"Don't be silly," her mother said. "Of course they'll come. Everybody can't have the flu."

"Wanna bet?" Kay said.

"What's going on here?" her father asked, joining them in the living room. "It's going to start pouring in a minute. Should I put the franks on now, or are we giving up on the barbecue idea?"

"We're giving up on it, Dad," Kay said.

"No we're not," her mother said. The phone rang again, and she picked it up immediately. "Hello, Mrs. Sloyer. Oh, I'm sorry to hear that. Yes, we certainly understand. Good-bye."

"The flu?" Kay asked.

"Her grandparents dropped by unexpectedly," her mother said.

"I hate them all," Kay said.

"I don't blame you," Jody said. "I feel like killing them."

"I don't understand," their father said. "Where is everybody?"

"Everybody's someplace else," Jody's mother declared. "Two mothers have called up with excuses, and frankly I'd be surprised if any of the others even bother doing that."

"They hate me," Kay said. "They only agreed to come because they felt sorry for me, and then they realized how much they hate me, so they all talked their mothers into letting them stay home."

"It isn't that bad, Kay," Jody said. "They don't hate you. They're just scared."

"What do they have to be scared about?" Kay cried. "That they'll come to my house and disappear?"

"I'm going to call all their mothers right now, and give them a piece of my mind," her mother said. "They can't treat my daughter this way."

"If you call them, I swear I'll never speak to you again," Kay said. "And I mean it." She ran upstairs and slammed her door.

"I'll talk to her," Jody said. "Mom, don't call. There's no point."

"I feel so helpless," her mother said and began to cry. The sound of her sobs was drowned out by the cloudburst outside.

"Great," Jody's father said. "All the barbecue stuff is still out there." He ran to the kitchen and Jody could hear him curse as he began bringing everything in.

Jody looked at her mother, thought about comforting her,

and then decided Kay came first. She went upstairs, knocked on Kay's door, and ignored her instructions to stay out.

"This really stinks," Jody said, sitting on the bed next to Kay.

"Tell me about it," Kay said.

Jody noticed Kay wasn't crying. There were no wads of tissues by the bed either.

"They're not afraid they're going to disappear," Jody said.

"I wish they would," Kay declared. "I wish everybody I know would disappear. Except maybe you."

Jody grinned. "Thanks for the exemption," she said.

"I said maybe," Kay pointed out. "Is Mom crying again?"

"What do you think?" Jody said.

"I don't see why she has to cry all the time," Kay said. "I'm not crying, and it's my birthday that's been ruined."

"She cries because she feels like a failure," Jody said. "Why aren't you crying?"

"Because I don't care anymore," Kay replied. "I'm never going to cry again."

"I won't hold you to that," Jody said. "You can even cry right now, and I won't call you a baby."

"I'm not a baby," Kay said, but she didn't whine it, the way she usually did. "I'm never going to be a baby again. I'm never going to be a baby, or cry, or have any friends ever again."

"Sounds good," Jody said. "Where do I sign up for lessons?"

"Your friends gave you a party," Kay said. "They talk to you."

"Not like they used to," Jody replied. "Except for Maris. And Maris would continue to complain if we were the last two people on earth."

"Nobody talks to me anymore," Kay said. "At lunch, they all get real busy when they see me coming. After school sometimes they actually run away from me."

"Kids your age can be cruel," Jody said.

"Fine," Kay said. "But they won't let me be cruel with them. I just get to be the victim all the time, and it isn't fair. I haven't done anything. Michael's the one who did, not me, so why do I have to be the victim?"

"They'll get over it," Jody said. "Your friends will come

around in time. You'll get invited to things again. You'll get to be cruel with everybody else."

"They can invite me, but I won't go," Kay said, clenching her fists. "I'm never going to talk to them again."

"You're going to have to have friends," Jody said. "Nobody can manage forever without them."

"I know that," Kay said. "And I'll have friends. Just not here."

"Where then?" Jody asked.

"I'm going to move in with Granny and Granddad," Kay said. "Nobody knows about Michael there."

"Are you serious?" Jody asked.

Kay nodded. "This was their last chance," she said. "If nobody showed up for my birthday party, then I decided I was going to leave here and move in with Gran."

"I don't suppose you've mentioned this to Mom and Dad," Jody said.

"I will tonight," Kay said. "When Mom is crying. She'll ask what she can do to make it up to me and I'll tell her."

"She'll never agree," Jody said. "She's already lost Michael. She isn't going to let you go too."

"I don't care," Kay said. "They don't love me anymore. They only love Michael. But I'll call Mom sometimes. And if Dad's still around, I'll talk to him too."

"Mom and Dad are not splitting up," Jody said. "If this past month hasn't done it, nothing will."

"Nothing is what's going to do it," Kay replied. "You want to come with me?"

"You're not going anywhere," Jody said. "Kay, you haven't mentioned this to Granny and Granddad, have you?"

Kay shook her head. "I'm going to call them now," she said. "They'll agree. Gran thinks Mom's responsible about Michael, I just know it."

"I'm sure you're right," Jody replied. "Gran always blames Mom for things. But that doesn't mean she wants a twelve-year-old living with her. I don't even think their retirement village allows kids to live there."

"Then they'll move," Kay said. "If I start crying and carrying on enough, they'll move so they can take me in. Granny would do anything I asked her to right now."

Jody looked at her sister in silent admiration. Kay had the situation pretty well sized up. If she played her cards right, she probably could get her grandparents to change all the details of their lives to take her in. And if Kay had the support of Granny and Granddad, then quite possibly her parents would agree to let her move in with them. It could be done with just the right kind of manipulation.

And Jody didn't blame Kay. If she could escape like that, get away from all the tension, she'd go too. Even if it did mean hurting everybody she cared about.

"You could come with me," Kay said. "We could share a room. If there's space for me, there's space for both of us."

"Oh, Kay," Jody said.

"Just until Michael gets back," Kay said. "Then we'll move back here, no matter how things are with Mom and Dad."

"Michael isn't coming back," Jody said.

"Oh?" Kay said. "You know something I don't?"

"That isn't what I mean," Jody said. "Of course Michael could still come back, he could come back this afternoon even, but we can't schedule things around it anymore. I've got to stop biting my nails right now, and not wait for Michael to come back. That's all I'm saying."

"Come with me," Kay said. "I know you want to."

"It isn't a question of what I want," Jody said. "It would kill Mom."

"Then stay," Kay said. "See if I care."

"You don't want to go without me," Jody said. "Think about it, Kay. Do you really want to have to deal with Granny all the time? She's okay in small doses, but on a full-time basis?"

"She's better than Mom," Kay said.

"Right now anybody's better than Mom," Jody replied. "But that's going to change too. It's only been six weeks since Michael left. Mom needs more time."

"She can have all the time in the world," Kay said. "Just as long as I'm not here."

"Kay, if you leave to live with Granny, you will never be my sister again," Jody said. She was startled by how cold the words sounded, and how cold she felt saying them.

"What?" Kay said.

69

"You heard me," Jody said. "No true sister would leave me to deal with Mom and Dad alone. And I can't go."

"You mean you'd never speak to me again?" Kay asked.

"I'd speak to you," Jody said. "I'd say hello and good-bye and thank you. If I had to, I'd even ask how you are. But I wouldn't listen and I wouldn't care. I'd be closer to Michael, even if he never came back, than I would be to you."

"I don't believe you," Kay said.

"Believe it," Jody replied. "Because if I did to you what you're threatening to do to me, you'd feel the exact same way."

"I'd move in with Granny and Granddad and be stuck with them, and you'd stay here and not like me anymore," Kay said. "What if I moved back here after a while?"

"Forget it," Jody said. "If you want to visit Granny for Thanksgiving or Christmas, that's fine. If you want me to come too, I'd be glad to. But you can't just disrupt their lives to please yourself and then change your mind and come back here and expect me to act as though you're still my sister. You know my terms. Stay here and I'll continue to love you. Move out, and you've lost me forever."

"I don't like you anymore," Kay said.

"Fine," Jody said. "It's mutual."

Kay stared at her sister, and then burst out crying. Jody smiled ruefully, and then held her sister close, not saying a word, hoping her embrace was language enough. Kay cried for fifteen minutes, and Jody silently handed her tissues, patted her back, brushed her hair back, and willed her to be all right.

"I'll stay," Kay said when she was in control enough to speak.

"I know," Jody said. "Thank you, Kay."

"But things have got to change," Kay said.

"They will," Jody said. "I promise." She got off the bed, giving Kay one final hug.

"I can't live like this," Kay said, and began crying again.

"You won't have to," Jody said. "I'll see to it you don't. It's the least a sister can do." She walked out of the room, closing the door behind her.

Downstairs her mother was sitting in the living room, under

70

the Happy Birthday sign. Her father was absently playing with a balloon.

"You're killing her," Jody said in the same cold voice she'd used with Kay. "The two of you are killing her."

"So what are we supposed to do?" Jody's father asked. "Force all her friends to come over? Pick up each and every one of them, so they can't possibly escape?"

"I made her the party she wanted," Jody's mother said. "The cake has lemon cream filling just the way she asked for."

"Have either of you even tried talking to her lately?" Jody asked. "Not about lemon cream. About her friends and how things are at school. About how she feels."

"We know how she feels," Jody's father said. "She feels the same way we all feel. Devastated. Helpless. No longer completely alive."

"Things will be better when Michael comes home," Jody's mother said.

"We can't wait that long," Jody said. "At least Kay can't."

"Jody, I know you love Kay, and I know you're trying to help," her father said. "But there's something you have to understand. What's happened to us, what's happening to us, won't just go away. We can love each other and communicate and give each other endless hugs and Michael will still be missing and we'll still be in hell. Kay isn't the only one slowly dying around here. We all are."

"But things have to get better," Jody said. "We can't keep on like this forever."

"Yes we can," her father replied. "Because frankly, we don't have any other choices."

71

Tuesday, November 12

"I'll set the table, Mom," Jody said, as her mother stood at the sink, scraping carrots for that night's salad.

"Thanks, dear," her mother said. "You're a big help."

Jody smiled. She walked over to the cabinet and took out four plates, then got out the same amount of silverware. It wasn't until she had reached the table and put the dishes down that she realized what she had done. Without even thinking about it, she had taken out four plates. No fifth plate for Michael. No thought of it, no little lurch inside. Just four plates, as though that was the norm.

Jody stared at the plates, the silverware, the table, all set up for four, and began to cry. Before her mother had a chance to ask why, she had run out of the kitchen in search of the sanctuary of her bedroom, to grieve at the fact that the unimaginable had become the norm.

Wednesday, November 20

As Jody left school that afternoon, she saw Jerry Murphy talking with a boy she recognized as someone Michael had known, but hadn't particularly liked. Brian Levine, she remembered. He and Michael had never gotten along.

Jerry and Brian were oblivious to the rest of the world, having an intense discussion that ended in a burst of laughter.

Jerry had been Michael's best friend, Jody thought. They'd been inseparable for years, and now Jerry was friends with someone Michael hadn't even liked.

Jody felt angry, then foolish, then angry again. It wasn't fair, she thought. Wherever Michael was, he still regarded Jerry as his best friend, but Jerry no longer needed Michael. Even that wasn't true. He was probably a lot happier forgetting all about Michael. He could amputate that part of his life and become friends with Brian Levine and be a normal fourteen-year-old boy again.

The anger turned to envy, and then all the feelings died and Jody walked away from Jerry, away from school, away from as much as she could.

Friday, November 22

"Guess what I heard today," Lauren said to Jody as they walked home after school.

"I give up," Jody replied. "What?"

"DeeDee Mackenzie is leaving town," Lauren declared. "Her father got transferred to Chicago. They're moving over Thanksgiving."

"So?" Jody said. "You and DeeDee aren't really friends."

"I swear your brain died," Lauren said. "DeeDee is a cheerleader. That means when she goes, there's going to be an opening on the squad."

"And you're going to try out?" Jody asked. "You never told me you wanted to be a cheerleader."

"I don't," Lauren said. "You do. Remember? It was all you talked about during the summer, how this year you were going to try out for the squad and how determined you were to make it. But then, well, nobody expected you to try out while all that stuff with Michael was going on. But now you can ask for a special tryout, and I'm sure you'll get it, and then you can make the squad."

"What makes you think I want to be a cheerleader anymore?" Jody asked.

"Because it was what you always wanted," Lauren replied. "And dreams like that don't just die."

Jody snorted.

"I don't like your attitude," Lauren said. "It isn't healthy. Jody, Michael's been gone for almost three months. It's about time you got on with your life."

"How can I?" Jody said. "What I'm living now isn't my life. It's a nightmare I've been dropped into."

"You know what I mean," Lauren declared. "And a good start would be if you tried out for cheerleader."

"The only cheers I have left are for Michael," Jody said. "Give me an *M*. Give me an *I*. Give me a Michael." She turned her face away from Lauren and willed herself not to cry.

"Michael wouldn't want you to live like this," Lauren said. "He'd want you to get on . . . he'd want you to be doing things, having a good time. He wouldn't want you to suffer all the time because of him."

"We can't really know that, can we?" Jody said. "If he's suffering right now, why should he want us to be happy? I'll be sure to ask him the next time he calls."

"Jody," Lauren said, but Jody had already begun trotting away from her, back to the refuge of her home, where everybody was stuck in the same nightmare, and they all knew there was nothing to cheer for.

Wednesday, November 27

"*H*ave a good time, girls," Jody's mother said at the airport. "Give our love to Granny and Granddad."

"I feel funny going off to Florida without you," Jody said to her mother. "We've never spent Thanksgiving apart."

"No matter what, we'd be spending it apart," her mother replied, "since Michael isn't here. Besides, your father and I will be fine. We'll have dinner tomorrow with Rob, and they'll watch all the football there is. That's all I can handle right now anyway. A big family celebration just wouldn't feel right."

"I don't know," Jody said.

"Jody, it's okay," Kay declared. "Mom'll be fine. Besides, Gran and Granddad need us now, don't they, Mom?"

"They're thrilled that you're coming," her mother replied. "And I know the two of you will behave yourselves and eat all that fine home cooking. Your grandmother loves to fuss over you, and right now you could both stand a little fussing."

"We'll be back on Sunday," Jody said. "Right, Kay?"

"Right," Kay said with a yawn. "Do you think they're going to board soon?"

"I'm sure they will," her mother said. "I shouldn't even be here; this area is just for passengers. So why don't I kiss both of you good-bye, and beat it before they send me away."

"I love you, Mom," Jody said, giving her mother a kiss. "Take it easy, all right?"

"Love you too," her mother said. "Come here, Kay. Give me a hug."

Kay walked over and reluctantly embraced her mother. "Bye, Mom," she said. "Have a happy Thanksgiving."

"You too," her mother said. "Come home tan, both of you."

"We'll do our best," Jody said, and gave her mother a final hug. Her mother looked at both of them for a moment, then smiled, and walked away.

Kay stared at her as she left. "Well, that could have been worse," she said. "But I'm glad it's over anyway."

Thursday, November 28

"*H*ave some more turkey."

"Gran, I couldn't eat another bite."

"She's too skinny," Jody's grandmother declared. "Isn't she, Harold? Both girls are. I bet you haven't eaten a thing in months what with everything that's been going on."

"We eat, Granny," Jody said. "Mom sees to that."

"It sure doesn't seem that way," her grandmother said. "Kay darling, have some more sweet potatoes."

"Sure, Gran," Kay said, passing her plate along. "Nobody cooks like you do, Granny."

"You hear that, Harold?" her grandmother crowed. "Kay knows good cooking when she tastes it."

"So do I, Angie," Jody's grandfather said. "I wouldn't turn down another helping myself."

"You're not going to have the chance to," Jody's grandmother replied. "The doctor says you have to lose ten more pounds, not gain. I told you you could have one helping of whatever you want today, seeing as it's Thanksgiving, but no seconds for you. Kay, have some more stuffing too."

"This is torture," Jody's grandfather said. "If all you're going to do is deprive me of food, then I'm leaving this table to watch some football."

"Fine," Jody's grandmother said. "We don't need you around anyway. We girls can entertain ourselves just fine, can't we, darlings?"

"Bye, Granddad," Jody said. Kay's mouth was too full to say anything.

"I'll be in the living room in case you change your mind," her grandfather declared. "About seconds, that is."

"You lose ten pounds, then I'll change my mind," Jody's grandmother replied. "And don't turn the set on too loud. We girls want to have a chance to chat."

Kay raised her eyebrows at Jody. Jody tried not to laugh. They had finally reached chat time.

"So, girls," Jody's grandmother said. "You poor children. Has it been very awful?"

"Yes," Jody said. There was no point lying about it. "We worry about Michael all the time."

"I pray for him every day," her grandmother declared. "And my church group prays regularly too. In my heart, I just know nothing bad has happened to him. A grandmother has ways of knowing these things. And Michael is so much like my Tom was at that age. Strong and self-reliant. Tommy was an Eagle Scout, you know."

"I know, Granny," Jody said. Kay kept on eating.

"Are you sure you wouldn't like something else?" Jody's grandmother asked. "Another biscuit maybe? I remembered that these are your favorites."

"I had three already, Gran," Jody said. "They were delicious."

"You poor girls," her grandmother said. "I know it isn't your mother's fault, her mother dying when she was so young and all, but she just never learned how to cook real home cooking, the kind Tommy loves so. It's no wonder the two of you are such skinny little things. I tried teaching Linda way back when she and Tommy were first married, but I don't think any of my lessons ever sunk in. I think you have to be brought up in a real happy home to learn how to cook the way I do. I know my mother taught me everything I know. These biscuits are my mama's recipe. Sure you wouldn't like another?"

"All right, Gran," Jody said. It was easier to give in and have some food to play with than to have to turn down offer after offer. Her grandmother lovingly handed her over the biscuit.

"There's gravy for it too, if you want," her grandmother said. "I can warm it right up for you."

"I don't need any, thanks," Jody said. "These biscuits are so good, they don't need gravy."

"Thank you, darling," her grandmother said. "Kay, it breaks my heart to see you eat like that."

"Like what, Gran?" Kay asked, putting her fork down nervously.

"It's as though you haven't eaten in months," her grandmother replied. "Are you sure your mother is making dinner for you every night?"

"Yes she is, Gran," Jody said.

"Well, I'm going to send a big package of food home with you girls on Sunday," her grandmother said. "And a couple of Tommy's favorite recipes as well. If your mother doesn't like it, then she can just lump it. That's what I say. Kay, would you like some more turkey? There's a lovely piece of white meat right here."

"No thanks," Kay said. "I want to save some space for pie."

"I baked three kinds," her grandmother declared. "Pecan and pumpkin and apple. And I expect you to try a slice of each one of them."

"Later," Jody said. She hadn't eaten that much in years, at least not since the last time her grandmother had had an occasion to cook. Her grandmother was a wonderful cook too, much better than her mother, but there was a limit, and Jody had passed hers several courses ago.

"I can't believe there's been no word from Michael," her grandmother said. "It's been over two months now, and not a clue as to his whereabouts."

"We know, Gran," Jody said.

"Your mother is a wonderful woman, please don't get me wrong," her grandmother said. "But sometimes when you're raised the way she was, not by your own mother, but by aunts and uncles, no mother's loving guidance, there's a lot about being a mother you simply never learn."

"Mom's a good mother," Jody said, glaring at Kay to make sure she didn't contradict her.

"Oh, of course she is," her grandmother said. "Of course she is, darling. But sometimes, how shall I put this, when a mother doesn't know just how to raise a child, especially a boy—boys can be the very devil sometimes—she overreacts to some little bit of mischief. There were times with Tommy and Robby I'd just be at wit's end, and if I hadn't had my own wonderful mother to turn to, I don't know what I would have done. Someday you'll both be mothers and you'll know what I mean."

"I'm never having kids," Kay declared.

"Don't say things like that, darling," her grandmother said. "Of course you will, beautiful children. They bring you joy nobody can ever take away from you."

"Someone took it away from Mom," Kay pointed out. "She isn't feeling joy anymore."

"But she will again," her grandmother said. "When Michael comes home. Jody darling, please don't take this the wrong way, but were there any problems between Michael and your mother? A fight maybe? Sometimes boys that age can be so rude, maybe your mother in the heat of anger struck him?"

"Mom's never hit any of us," Jody declared. "Ever."

"You don't always know what happens between a mother and child," her grandmother said.

"If I wouldn't know, then why ask me?" Jody replied.

"I knew you would take it the wrong way," her grandmother said. "Jody darling, even the best mother in the world loses control sometimes."

"Mom didn't lose control," Jody said.

"Then maybe Michael felt constricted at home," her grandmother said. "A growing boy, he wants his freedom. Your mother, does she still kiss Michael each night when he goes to bed?"

"Not anymore she doesn't," Kay said. Jody kicked her under the table.

"Granny, you can't have it both ways," Jody said. "Either you think Michael ran away because Mom was beating up on him, or else you think he ran away because Mom was too affectionate. But you have to choose."

"How can I choose?" her grandmother asked. "I live a thousand miles away. I don't see what goes on in your household. I only know what I'm told."

"I didn't know Michael ran away," Kay said. "Mom doesn't think he did."

"None of us know what became of Michael," Jody said. "I don't think he ran away either."

"It's just the other possibilities," her grandmother said with a shudder. "Some man taking him for God knows what."

"He might have been murdered," Kay said. "Well, he might have been. We don't know."

"Michael isn't dead," Jody said automatically.

"I wish you'd stop saying that," Kay said. "You always say it as though you had some kind of proof. We don't know. Michael could be lying in a ditch right now, or buried in some forest. We don't know."

"God would never do that to my Michael," her grandmother said.

"I don't know why not," Kay replied. "He's done it to lots of other boys. I know. I've been reading articles. There are these murderers who love to kill boys, and they trap them and murder them and bury their bodies where nobody can find them. Someone like that could have found Michael. Michael could have been dead for the past two months, when every time the phone rings or someone knocks on the door we all stop everything and somebody whispers 'Michael' and we expect him to come right in as though nothing happened. That would be some joke, all right. All of us waiting for Michael to come home, and he's cut up into a hundred little pieces somewhere buried under somebody's cellar floor."

"Kay, don't speak that way!" her grandmother said. "Jody, tell her to stop."

"Oh, Gran," Jody said. "It's what we all think, only none of us have the courage to say it. We can't say it in front of Mom or Dad, and they can't say it to us either, so we just think it and worry about it and think it some more. I'm glad Kay said it and I'm glad she said it here. You're right, Kay. Maybe Michael is dead. I don't know any more than you do."

"This is all your mother's fault," Jody's grandmother declared. "What happened to Michael, the way you girls are behaving, this is all Linda's doing."

"Daddy was the one who wasn't home when Michael disappeared," Kay said. "Your precious Tommy was the one hiding out at the cabin. Don't blame Mom for everything. Daddy was just as much at fault."

Jody's grandmother began crying at the table. Jody stared at her and at her sister. She didn't blame Kay for behaving the way she did, but that didn't make things any easier.

"Gran, we're all worried sick," Jody said. "You have to understand that."

"Don't you think I'm worried too?" her grandmother asked. "We feel so helpless down here. We offered to come up when Michael first disappeared, but Tommy told us not to, he said there wasn't anything we could do. We knew that. But we're the boy's grandparents. We want to be something more than just another name on the list of people to call with updates. I thought if you could only tell me something you couldn't tell anyone else, something about how Michael was getting along with his mother, then maybe we could figure out where he went to, and we could find him before something awful did happen to him."

"Granny, there aren't any clues," Jody said. "Don't you think we've tried? We've gone over everything again and again. We've searched his room, talked to his friends, looked for any little something that might lead us to him. The police have looked too, and there just isn't anything. We don't know any more about where Michael is than we did on Labor Day. He's just gone, and all we can hope for is that somehow he'll manage to get back to us."

"He's my only grandson," Jody's grandmother sobbed. "I miss him so much."

"I know, Granny," Jody said. "We all do. We all miss Michael all the time."

Friday, November 29

"You're the Chapman girls, aren't you?" a blue-haired lady asked them, as Jody and Kay sat by the pool. "Harold and Angie's grandchildren."

"That's right," Jody replied.

"Oh, you poor children," the woman said. "What a tragedy."

"Thank you," Kay said.

"If there's anything I can do," the lady said. "Your grandparents are such lovely people. The pain they've had to endure. We've all suffered with them, I want you to know that. Their pain has been our pain."

"We appreciate that," Jody said. Kay coughed, a sure sign of an incipient giggle attack. "Come on, Kay, I'll race you the length of the pool."

"You're on," Kay said, jumping in. Jody followed her and allowed the soothing sensation of making muscles work to comfort her. Kay had been wrong. Even in Florida, people knew all about Michael.

"I think we should change our names," Kay said, as the girls treaded water following their race. "To O. U. Poor Children. That's all we get called around here anyway."

"At least they're talking to you," Jody pointed out. "Maybe you should move down here, Kay. Think of all the new friends you'd make. All those lovely people who are suffering right along with you."

"Nah, I've changed my mind," Kay said. "I couldn't live with Granny's cooking. It's a miracle Granddad only needs to lose ten pounds."

"He's already lost twenty," Jody said. "All since September."

"Mom's lost that much too," Kay said. "Have you noticed, she's hardly eating anymore."

"I've noticed," Jody said. "I didn't think you had."

"When you were twelve, did Mom drive you crazy?" Kay asked.

Jody thought about it. "I wanted to murder her," she said. "Sometimes just being in the same room with her made me want to puke."

"Fine," Kay said. "Then think about how you felt and multiply it by a thousand. Because Mom is at least a thousand times crazier than she was four years ago."

"All right," Jody said. "You've made your point. Just remember though, Mom has reason to be crazy."

"As if I could forget," Kay replied. "Jody, do you think Michael really is dead?"

"I don't know what to think," Jody replied. "I sure hope not."

"Sometimes I wish he was," Kay said. "Sometimes I wish they'd call us up and say they've found his body. Is that wrong of me? I worry that maybe it's a sin to want that."

"I don't think you want Michael to be dead," Jody said, picking her words carefully. "I think you just want to know where he is, what's become of him. It's not the same thing."

"I'd rather he was dead and we knew it than alive with things staying the way they are," Kay declared. "I've never told that to anybody but it's true."

"It doesn't matter what you want," Jody said. "We all want to know where Michael is, but that doesn't mean we're about to find out. It isn't something we have any control over."

"I don't think we have control over anything anymore," Kay said. "If we did, I'd still have friends, and I wouldn't be flunking half my subjects, and Granddad would weigh ten pounds less."

"What do you mean you're flunking half your subjects?" Jody asked, getting out of the pool. Kay followed her and they toweled themselves off.

"It's okay," Kay said. "Nobody's going to fail me, not this semester. But I haven't passed a math test all year, and I've flunked most of my spelling tests as well, and my science tests too. A couple of my teachers have tried talking with me, but I just start crying, and they get all flustered and leave me alone."

"Oh, Kay," Jody said.

"Don't 'Oh, Kay' me," Kay said. "How are you doing in school?"

"Not great," Jody admitted. "My average is about to go down ten points."

"Your grades are more important than mine," Kay said. "You're a junior. Your grades count for things. You have to keep your grades up, if you want to get a scholarship."

"Maybe I won't need one," Jody said.

"Why not?" Kay asked. "Because Mom and Dad won't have to pay for Michael's education?"

"Don't say things like that," Jody said. "It's a jinx."

Kay looked at her sister and laughed. "You were the one

who said we don't have any control," she pointed out. "How can I possibly jinx things?"

"You can't," Jody said. "But let's not risk it. All right?"

"Whatever you say," Kay replied, and jumping back into the pool, she languidly began swimming away from her sister.

Sunday, December 1

The girls paid for headsets on the flight home and listened contentedly to the canned music the airplane provided. Jody stared over Kay's head, out the window, and looked down upon the clouds. She wondered if that was what the souls of people looked like after they'd died, free-floating, vaporous clouds.

Kay tapped her on the shoulder. "I don't want to go home," she said.

"Neither do I," Jody admitted. "Not really. But we don't have any choice in the matter."

"I know," Kay said. "I was crazy to think I could live with Granny and Granddad."

Jody nodded.

"Do you think we can go away for Christmas too?" Kay asked.

"You mean back to Granny's?" Jody replied.

"Anywhere," Kay said. "Anywhere that isn't home."

Jody shrugged. "You can ask," she said. "But Mom isn't going to like it."

"Do you know what it's going to be like at home for Christmas?" Kay said. "If Michael isn't back by then."

"I don't even want to think about it," Jody said.

"Only twenty-four more days," Kay said. "I think you'd better start thinking."

"It can wait," Jody said, staring out at the clouds. "Besides, maybe Michael will be back by then."

"Sure," Kay said. "Maybe Santa Claus will bring him back to us."

"We can hope," Jody said.

"You can hope," Kay said. "I'm not hoping for anything ever again."

Jody looked at her sister and realized Kay meant it. She sighed and turned away from her. Hope wasn't much, but it was all she had left, and she wasn't ready to give it up just yet. Michael might be back by Christmas, she told herself. They didn't know where he was, so there was no reason to assume he wouldn't be back by then. If Michael was home by Christmas, then everything would be all right again.

Tuesday, December 3

*T*hey sat around the kitchen table, eating their supper in the strained silence Jody had come to associate with home and meals and evenings. Her father cleared his throat and they all looked up at him, startled by the noise, and eager to see if words might follow.

"Your mother and I have something to tell you," he said.

They're getting a divorce, Jody thought, and she couldn't tell what she felt—shock, sorrow, or relief.

Her father pushed his plate away from him. "We've decided to let a private investigator look into this business with Michael," he said. "To look for him, I mean."

"Then Gran talked Granddad into it," Kay said. "Good for her."

"What?" Jody said.

"How do you know about it?" her mother asked Kay.

"I was just down there, Mom," Kay said. "Gran talked to me about it. About what she could do, and I said how about hiring a detective. It isn't like the police have done anything, and

Gran and Granddad have money, and somebody's got to do something."

"This was your idea?" her mother asked.

"Not exactly," Kay said. "It's just kids at school kept asking me why you didn't hire a detective, like on TV, to find Michael, and Gran was desperate to do something, so I mentioned it. I don't know why you haven't suggested it to them."

"Because I don't want to see my parents wasting their money," her father replied. "Which will probably happen."

"Your father seems to think your grandparents' bank account is more important than his son," Jody's mother declared.

"Linda," Jody's father said with a sigh. "We talked about hiring a detective back in October," he said to his daughters. "But the police said it would be a waste of money. Of course, they were still saying Michael would be back any day now. They said if we put Michael's name and picture down on the missing children's lists, let all the organizations, public and private, know about him, we had as good a chance of finding him as any detective. And we chose to listen to them."

"*You* chose," Jody's mother said. "And we've wasted those months and God knows how Michael has suffered. But all right. What's done is done. Gran and Granddad at least have come to their senses, and something's going to get done. Let's just pray it isn't too late."

"We all pray that every night," Jody's father said. "You're not the only one, Linda, who prays for that."

"If I'd had the money, I would have hired the detective myself," Jody's mother said. "But not all of us have the good fortune to have wealthy parents."

"If you hadn't quit your job, you could have used your salary to pay for the damn detective," Jody's father declared. "But you'd rather get into power plays, see if we can force my parents into doing it. Well, it worked, and they've offered, and the detective is coming on Thursday evening to talk to all of us. That's why we're telling you. We want both of you to be here Thursday, so we can all talk to him. All right?"

Jody started laughing.

"What's so funny?" Kay asked.

"We're always here," Jody replied. "Dad doesn't have to

86

tell us to be here. Michael's gone, but the rest of us are here all the time." She continued to laugh.

"I fail to see what's funny," her mother said, but that didn't stop Jody from laughing, and soon Kay was laughing with her. The two sat at the kitchen table as their dinners grew cold, laughing at the idea of ever being somewhere else, laughing at their parents, who no longer remembered anything about laughing.

Thursday, December 5

*J*ohn Grainger didn't look like any of the detectives Jody had seen on television, but that didn't bother her as she sat in the living room looking him over. He looked more like a retired police officer, which, it turned out, was exactly what he was.

"I want you all to understand I make no guarantees," he said, sitting in the easy chair, his body leaning forward so he could look at all of them more closely. "The odds at this point of one person finding Michael are very, very small."

"We know that," Jody's mother said. "But we have to do something. Everything else has failed."

"Not necessarily," Mr. Grainger replied. "It simply hasn't worked yet. And if Michael did leave of his own volition, then he could decide to make contact at any time. Of course, that's what we're all hoping for."

"But if Michael didn't run away," Jody's mother said. "And if he isn't . . . if he needs our help . . ."

"There's no way of knowing," Mr. Grainger said. "Which is the hell you people have had to live with. What I can do for you is go over the track one more time, see if I can dig up a witness who might remember having seen Michael. I can also look over the current kiddie porn literature. Michael's a good-looking kid, and young for his age. That makes him natural prey. I can put feelers out, ask some questions, see if I can find out anything. It isn't like the movies. I'm not going to find half a shoelace and solve the mystery. And you all have to be prepared that I might not find anything, and you also have to be prepared that if I do find something, it might be bad news. Very bad news. The odds are at this point there won't be any good news."

"Even if Michael ran away?" Jody asked.

"Even if he ran away," Mr. Grainger replied. "He's been gone three months now. Three months is an eternity for a runaway. Not much good happens to a runaway."

"We don't care," Jody's mother said. "We want Michael back, no matter what he's been through."

"We need to know how he is," Jody's father said. "We'll be grateful for anything you can find out."

"Fine," Mr. Grainger said. "Now, Mr. and Mrs. Chapman, I hope you won't be offended, but I'd like some time alone with your daughters. Then I'll talk with both of you some more. All right?"

"Certainly," Jody's father said. "Come on, Linda. Let's go to our room and get those pictures."

"The girls won't have anything to tell you they couldn't say in front of us," Jody's mother said. "We don't have any secrets."

"I'm sure," Mr. Grainger said. "But it's hard to interview four people at once. Two and two should make things easier. All right?"

"Fine," Jody's father said. "Come on, Linda. Give him a chance."

Jody's parents left the living room. Jody could see how reluctant her mother was to be parted from Mr. Grainger and the hope, however slight, that he offered.

"So, Jody, I hear you were the last one in the family to see Michael," Mr. Grainger said, relaxing in the chair.

Jody nodded. "He was on his way to Jerry Murphy's to play softball," she said for the thousandth time. "I was going to the movies with my friend Maris."

"And you talked about the possibility your parents might be getting a divorce," Mr. Grainger said.

Jody nodded. "But he didn't say anything about running away," she declared. "We just talked. He said he'd be home in time for supper."

"I have a question," Kay said.

"Sure," Mr. Grainger said.

"If you find out he's dead, will you tell us?" Kay asked.

"You get right to the heart of the matter, don't you, kid?" Mr. Grainger said. "Of course I'll tell you. That's why I've been hired."

"So we'd know," Kay said. "I mean, you wouldn't just tell Gran and Granddad because they're paying you, and then if they didn't want us to know, they wouldn't tell us."

"I'd tell your parents first," Mr. Grainger replied. "That's the arrangement I made with your grandparents. They're paying me, but my report will go directly to your parents. Why? Do you have some reason to believe Michael is dead?"

Kay shook her head. "Jody saw him last," she said. "I was out with Mom shopping."

Mr. Grainger smiled at her. "I didn't think you'd killed him," he said to Kay. "I wasn't asking for an alibi."

"Sometimes I feel . . ." Kay began, but then she shut up.

"Let me ask you another question," Mr. Grainger said. "Do you feel that your grandparents might know something they're not saying?"

"Of course not," Jody said. "What could they possibly know?"

"Kay, how do you feel?" Mr. Grainger asked, and Jody blushed. Mr. Grainger obviously didn't care about her opinion one bit. "Did your grandmother say something to you when you were down there for Thanksgiving?"

Kay shook her head. "I asked her," she said, "if maybe Michael had called her, you know, since he's been gone, and she said of course not. So then I asked her if maybe Michael had called her that weekend, Labor Day, because he's really close to Gran, and sometimes he likes to talk to her more than to anybody else. And she said no, he hadn't, and then she started to cry, and she said there'd been a message on her answering machine, he'd called on Saturday, but she and Granddad were out all day and they didn't get back until late that night, and when they called Sunday afternoon, nobody answered. She cried a lot."

"I don't believe this," Jody said. "When did she tell you all this?"

89

"Saturday night," Kay replied. "After you'd gone to sleep. I had a bad dream and I woke up and went into the kitchen, and Gran was there, because she's having trouble sleeping lately too. She said Granddad didn't even know. He hates the answering machine, so she doesn't bother telling him about messages, and she's sure if she'd called Sunday morning, she would have spoken to Michael and everything would have been different."

"I see," Mr. Grainger said.

"That doesn't mean anything," Jody said. "So he left a message and Gran never told anybody. Did he say anything on the message?"

"Not really," Kay replied. "She kept the tape and she made me listen to it." She shuddered. "It was really weird, hearing his voice like that. He sounded okay though. Just like Michael."

"This is all very interesting," Mr. Grainger declared. "Did your grandmother say anything else that night, Kay?"

"Just how sorry she was," Kay replied. "She said that a lot. How sorry she was and that it was her fault because she hadn't called back. I said it wasn't her fault, because it wasn't, but she didn't listen to me. Nobody does."

"I will," Mr. Grainger promised.

"Then could you please not tell Mom," Kay said. "She and Gran fight all the time anyway, and Mom'll blame Gran, and then she and Dad will fight, and somehow everybody'll decide it's all my fault."

Jody looked at her sister and realized everything she had said was true. "Kay has a point," she said. "Mom's on edge lately. She does blame other people for things."

"When I talk to your grandmother about the tape, I'll suggest to her she tell your mother," Mr. Grainger said. "How's that?"

"All right," Kay said.

"Now let me ask both of you if you think Michael ran away," Mr. Grainger said. "Jody?"

"I don't know anymore," Jody replied. "I used to be sure he didn't, and then I hoped he had, and now I just don't know. All I can tell you is he seemed perfectly normal when I talked to him on Sunday. I just wish we knew where he was."

90

"What do you think, Kay?" Mr. Grainger asked. "Did Michael say anything to you that weekend?"

"Michael never said anything to me," Kay replied. "He just called me baby all the time and told me to stop whining."

Mr. Grainger smiled. "It can be rough being the youngest," he said. "But you seem like a smart girl, Kay. You must have some thoughts about Michael, where he is."

"I think he's dead," Kay replied.

"Kay!" Jody said sharply.

"Well, I do," Kay said. "I know I'm not supposed to, but that's what I think. And if he is, then I hope you can find out, Mr. Grainger, and tell us so we'll know. Okay?"

"I'll do my best," Mr. Grainger said. "I promise you that, Kay."

"Thank you," Kay said. "Because I don't know how much more of this I can stand."

Tuesday, December 10

"*I* don't believe Christmas is only two weeks away," Lauren said, as she, Jody, and Maris finished eating their lunches. "I still have to do half my shopping."

"I'm all through shopping," Maris declared, twirling her straw wrapper around her ring finger. "I bought Mom a real sexy nightgown."

"You didn't," Lauren said. "My mother would die if I got her anything like that."

"Your mother has less use for it than mine," Maris replied. "It's black, and it's see-through, and it kind of has feathers. I don't think they're real feathers though, because it was pretty cheap. It looks pretty cheap too, which is just the way my mother likes 'em."

"I'm getting my mother a book," Lauren said. "Something without any sex in it. And I'm getting my father a pipe."

"I thought your father smoked cigars," Maris said.

"He does," Lauren replied. "But pipes are so much nicer. Maybe if I give him one, he'll switch over."

"Good thinking," Maris said. "Maybe I should give my mother a nun's habit and see if that makes a difference."

"I don't know what I'm giving my parents yet," Jody said. "I know the one thing they want, and it's something I can't buy them."

"Everybody loves presents," Maris declared. "Get them something big and expensive and it'll take their minds off of Michael."

Jody laughed. "Nothing will do that," she said. "I could buy them the Statue of Liberty, and all they'd think about would be Michael."

"I think about him a lot too," Lauren said. "Sometimes I remember what a pest he could be, and how I'd snap at him, try to get him away from us, and I feel terrible. I did like him. Do you think he knew that, Jody?"

"I don't think he cared," Maris said.

"I wasn't asking you," Lauren said. "Jody, do you think Michael knew I liked him?"

"I'm sure he did," Jody said. "Does. I'm sure Michael didn't mind. He was a pest sometimes."

"He was a pest all the time," Maris said. "I like Kay though. What are you getting her for Christmas?"

"She told me not to get her anything," Jody said. "She said she just wants money this year."

"You can't give a twelve-year-old money for Christmas," Lauren declared. "What are you going to do? Gift wrap a ten-dollar bill?"

"If that's what the kid wants, why not give it to her?" Maris asked. "Maybe Kay is saving up for something big, like a computer or a horse. She's too young for a car."

"I asked her what she wanted the money for," Jody said. "She just said she wanted to build up her savings account. I feel bad not trusting her, but I wish I knew what she had in mind."

"It's probably something about Michael," Maris said. "That's all any of you have had on your minds for months now."

"I know," Jody said. "And if Michael isn't back by New Year's, then I'm making a resolution to change that."

92

"How?" Lauren asked.

"I don't know yet," Jody replied. "But I can't let Michael dominate my thoughts all the time. I've got to start thinking about school and friends and living again."

Lauren smiled at Jody. "Maybe Michael will be back by then," she said. "And then you won't have to make any resolutions."

"Maybe," Jody said. "But starting with New Year's, I swear it isn't going to matter anymore."

Thursday, December 12

"*I* want to talk to you girls about something," Jody's mother declared after they had gotten home from school.

"Sure, Mom," Jody said, taking an apple out of the refrigerator. "What's up?"

"You too, Kay," her mother said. "This concerns both of you."

"I'm listening," Kay said. "Can't I get a glass of milk?"

"Of course you can," her mother said. "Pour your milk and sit down so we can talk."

Kay grimaced, but followed her mother's instructions. Jody took a bite out of the apple and waited for her mother to begin.

"I want to talk to you about Christmas," Jody's mother declared when the girls had settled in. "It's less than two weeks away."

"We know that, Mom," Kay said. "Can we go now?"

"You'll go when I say you can go," her mother declared. "Now Christmas has always been a very important holiday for this family, and there's no reason why things should be any different this year. Your father's buying a tree this weekend, and we'll expect you both to help us decorate it, the same as we always do."

"I want to go to Florida for Christmas," Kay said. "To see Granny and Granddad."

"You can't," her mother replied. "We're spending Christmas together as a family. Which leads me to the next order of business."

"What, Mom?" Jody asked. Kay seemed too stunned to start whining.

"I expect both of you to buy presents for Michael," her mother announced.

"What?" Kay screeched. "Mom, Michael isn't here anymore. Remember?"

"He may well be back for Christmas," her mother said. "I spoke to Officer Dino about it at Thanksgiving and he said lots of times missing kids show up at holidays. Their . . . the people they're with take pity on them and they're allowed to go home."

"Mom, that's a crock," Kay said. "I bet he said runaways get homesick for their presents and that's why they show up."

"He said both," her mother declared. "Now, whatever the reason, I think we should all assume Michael will be back at Christmastime. And think how disappointed he'd be if he came home and there were no presents waiting for him. Your father and I are buying him the computer he was always talking about."

"Mom, that's crazy," Kay said. "It costs hundreds of dollars. Michael could be dead. You don't spend that kind of money on a dead person."

"Don't you ever say that again!" her mother shouted. "He's not dead. Do you hear me? Michael is not dead, and he deserves as much love as he always did. More. The computer is what he always wanted, and now he's going to get it. When Michael comes home, he's going to find that computer under the tree. Along with presents from you. Is that clearly understood?"

"Jody," Kay pleaded.

"Mom, a computer costs a lot of money," Jody said. "And you're not working anymore. Couldn't you just put the money away someplace, and when Michael comes home, you could go shopping with him for the computer?"

"And have him find a bankbook under the tree?" her mother asked. "What kind of present is that for a thirteen-year-old?"

"Fourteen," Kay said. "He's fourteen now, remember?"

"A fourteen-year-old," her mother said. "Honestly, girls, I never expected you to be so selfish. You maybe, Kay. You've never cared about this family. It's always been, 'What can I get for myself?' But Jody, I expected better of you."

"I hate you," Kay said.

"Fine," her mother said. "Hate me. I don't care. Just buy Michael something nice for Christmas."

Kay stared at her mother as she got up from the table.

"Something very nice," her mother said. "If you want to get any Christmas presents from us, then you'd better buy something for Michael." She walked out of the kitchen.

Kay threw her milk glass across the room. It crashed against the refrigerator, splattering milk and pieces of broken glass across the floor.

"She hates me," Kay said. "Doesn't she, Jody?"

"Maybe she does," Jody said. "Right now, anyway. Don't bother about the mess, Kay. I'll clean it up."

Wednesday, December 18

"So what did you end up getting Michael?" Maris asked after school as they stood by their lockers.

"I bought him a book about baseball cards," Jody said. "He still has his collection, so I figured he'd like it."

"Besides, it won't go bad," Maris said. "In case it has to sit under the tree for a while. And did you decide what to give Kay?"

Jody sighed. "I'm giving her just what she asked for. A ten-dollar bill all nicely gift-wrapped."

"Do you think she's planning to buy a one-way ticket with it?" Maris asked.

"I don't know," Jody replied. "But if she is, I just may go along with her."

Wednesday, December 25

"The sweater's beautiful, Mom," Jody said. "I love the color."

"I knew it would look good on you," her mother replied. "The green brings out the hazel in your eyes."

"And do you like the watch?" her father asked.

"I love it," Jody said. "I've been looking at watches just like it. How did you know?"

"I didn't," her father said. "It was just a guess on my part. Kay, how do you like your presents?"

"They're fine, Dad," Kay replied. "But why did you get me a doll? I'm too old for dolls."

"I picked it out," her mother said. "You told me you wanted a doll just like that."

"When I was nine," Kay said. "Not anymore."

"You can always return it," her mother said.

"Maybe I will," Kay said. "Do you think they'd give me money for it?"

"Speaking of money, why in heaven's name did you give Kay money for Christmas?" Jody's mother asked her. "Couldn't you think of anything more appropriate?"

"I didn't have time to shop," Jody said. "I've really been studying hard lately, to try to get my grades up before the semester ends."

"Hear that, Kay?" her mother said. "That's the kind of example you should follow."

"Fine," Kay said. "The blouse is nice. Thank you, Dad."

"I hope I got the size right," he said. "Your mother usually shops with me when I get you girls clothes, but we couldn't get together this year."

"I know," Kay said. "It's hard to find the time now that she isn't working."

96

"Nobody appreciates your sarcasm, Kay," her mother said. "Anyone care for another glass of eggnog?"

"Not me," Jody said, looking at the tree. Michael's gifts remained conspicuously wrapped. The computer took up most of the room, but there were a couple of smaller boxes from her parents, and the book she'd bought, and something she assumed came from Kay. The tree usually looked festive when there were unopened boxes under it, but this year it just seemed like a sham.

"What a lovely gift from Lauren," Jody's mother said. "A journal, so you can write all your thoughts down."

"Yes, it is nice," Jody said, knowing she would never use it. The kinds of thoughts she'd been having were best left unwritten.

"If we're through with all this gift-giving stuff, then I'm going upstairs," Kay declared. "So I can play with my dolly in peace."

"Go," her mother said.

Kay scowled and left her presents downstairs. Jody watched her for a moment, then looked down at her hands. Her fingernails were all bitten again. Starting on New Year's, she told herself. On New Year's things will get back to normal. In one week's time. That's all she needed. Just one more week.

Wednesday, January 1

*J*ody woke up at five that morning and lay on her bed, thinking about the new year. True, Michael wasn't home, and there was still no clue as to where he was. But he'd been gone for four months, and life had to resume sometime. That's what new years were invented for, to give you the excuse to start fresh.

The first step, she knew, was to return some kind of normalcy to her family. Jody knew the damage done between her mother and Kay was beyond her abilities to repair, but there were other things she could do, things no one else in the family was equipped for. And the first would take only a few minutes, and was best done while everyone else was sleeping.

So she tiptoed downstairs and went to the living room. The tree still stood proudly in the corner, starting to shed its needles, but still looking good. And Michael's presents remained under it as they had for over a week, gaily wrapped and ribboned. It hadn't been easy keeping Baron from those ribbons, but Jody's mother had managed, and if Michael walked in right then, he'd find his presents exactly as they were on Christmas Eve.

Jody looked at the door, the way she always did when she thought about Michael coming home, but as always, there was no Michael. One of these days, she thought, Michael actually would show up, and she'd probably die from the shock. Let's see what that would do to the family. She laughed the new grim laugh she'd acquired.

The computer weighed the most, and it was the first present she took upstairs. She carried it carefully, not caring to think about the disaster that would follow if she dropped it on the stairs. Grunting quietly, she carried it to Michael's room, and put it first on his desk, and then in his closet. Baron stared at her from Michael's bed, so Jody closed the closet door to keep him away from it.

She went back downstairs and was able to gather up the rest of Michael's gifts and carry them all together. Again she rested them on Michael's desk, so she could open the closet door. Baron yawned mightily, and stretched one paw out before falling back asleep.

Jody looked around her brother's room and prayed with all her might that he might return one day to it. She opened the closet door and started putting the presents in there, piling them up carefully by size.

When she got to Kay's present, however, she couldn't resist. She had no idea what Kay had bought Michael, only knew that she'd shown up with a beautifully wrapped box and a large Christmas card. Jody slid the ribbon off the box, and then carefully removed the paper, making sure not to tear anything. Michael might not care if Jody snooped around his things, but she suspected her mother might. It was just the kind of thing that set her mother off these days, and the last thing Jody wanted was a confrontation with her mother.

She put the paper aside and then opened the box. Inside was some tissue paper, and she removed it, looked in, and saw Kay had given her brother a beautifully gift-wrapped rock. From the looks of it, it came from her mother's rock garden.

Jody picked the rock up and laughed. Kay had taken a gamble, but she probably figured she had nothing to lose. And whatever else you were going to say about a rock, it wouldn't go bad, no matter how long it sat waiting to be admired.

Jody put the rock back in its box, rewrapped the gift, slipped the ribbon back on, and put the box behind the box with the computer. She closed the closet door quietly, walked over to Michael's bed to scratch Baron's chin, and then went back to her bedroom, climbed into her own bed, and fell into a long, dreamless sleep.

LAUGHING IN
THE DARK

Monday, January 13

"*You Can't Take It With You!*" Maris cried in disgust, as she, Jody, Lauren, and dozens of other juniors jostled to get a better look at the bulletin board. "What do they think this is, 1957?"

"More like 1937," Lauren said. "*You Can't Take It With You* is a classic from the thirties."

"I don't care if it's a classic from the twenty-first century," Maris grumbled as she walked away. Her place was immediately taken by four other juniors. "They never give the junior class anything interesting to do for their class play."

"Last year they did *Arsenic and Old Lace,*" Jody said, walking off with Maris and Lauren.

"And the year before that I bet they did *You Can't Take It With You,*" Maris declared. "And next year, they'll probably do *Arsenic and Old Lace.* Those are the only two plays they know around here."

"It isn't so bad for the seniors," Lauren said. "They did *West Side Story* last year, and this year I think they're going to be doing *The Sound of Music.*"

"Singing nuns, great," Maris said. "I'll be sure to take my mother to see that one."

"I'm trying out," Jody declared. "How about the two of you?"

Maris shook her head. "I'm holding out for singing nuns," she said. "I refuse to be in any play that doesn't have a singing nun."

"I can't act," Lauren said. "I'll see if they need me on one of the committees. Props maybe, or costumes."

"You could do that too, Maris," Jody said. "You'd be great at publicity."

103

"Too wholesome," Maris said. "I've decided to follow my mother's lead and devote this semester to throwing myself at boys."

"Any boys in particular?" Jody asked.

"Seniors preferably," Maris replied. "With their own cars and bad reputations."

"Great," Lauren said. "Just don't expect me to throw the baby shower."

"There isn't going to be a baby shower," Maris said. "I haven't watched my mother in action all these years for nothing. I'm just ready to be wild. Almost seventeen is the best time for wildness."

"You aren't going to be seventeen for another seven months," Lauren declared. "That's hardly almost."

"It's going on almost," Maris said. "Anyway, it's close enough. Jody, want to become wild with me?"

"I don't think so," Jody replied. "Thanks for the invitation though. I'm going to try out for the play and do lots of extra assignments to bring my grades up. Maybe next year I'll be wild."

"Next year I'll be beyond wild," Maris said. "When are you going to be wild, Lauren? Before or after you turn eighty?"

"After," Lauren said with a sigh. "Well, you might as well be realistic about these things. I'm not a fast mover, and wild isn't going to come naturally to me."

"I'll give you lessons," Maris said. "With my help, you should reach wild sometime before your sixtieth birthday."

"Great," Lauren replied. "I'd love to be wild while I still have all my own teeth."

Jody laughed. "Can I sit in on the lessons?" she asked. "I don't think I was born to be wild either."

"I may have to open up a school," Maris said. "Jeez. How can I be wild if I'm a teacher? Forget it, both of you. You're on your own."

"Don't be too wild," Jody said. "Wild within limits."

"Yes, Mother," Maris said and giggled.

Jody laughed along with her and soon Lauren joined in. They walked out of the school together, still laughing, no longer caring why.

Thursday, January 16

"Very good, Jody," Mr. Lucas said. "Now if you could just read the next speech the same way you read that one. Naturally, as though you were having a conversation."

"I'll try," Jody replied, and skimmed the speech one more time. She'd read it over and over while the other kids were trying out, but it had been distracting, especially since she wasn't sure just who her character was supposed to be. She'd tried to get her hands on a copy of the play, but they were all taken out of the school and public libraries. Apparently she hadn't been the only one to come up with that idea.

"I'll read Tony's lines," Mr. Lucas said. " 'Besides, darling, we're not going to live with our families. It's just you and I.' "

Jody took a deep breath. " 'No, it isn't—' " she read, trying to look up from the paper as much as she could. " 'It's never quite that. I love them, Tony—I love them deeply.' " She kept on reading from her sheet, pausing when Mr. Lucas read his lines, and then continuing as Alice, who seemed to have family problems all her own.

"Very good, Jody," Mr. Lucas said when she'd finished. "Thank you very much."

"You're welcome," Jody said. "Thank you."

"Next," Mr. Lucas said, and Jody walked off the stage, using the back staircase.

"Want to bet she gets the part?" she heard one girl whisper to another.

"She was good," the second girl whispered back.

"That doesn't matter," the first girl said. "They'll give it to her because they're all so sorry for her."

Jody felt as though someone had punched her, and then, when the pain lessened, she realized she didn't care why they gave her the part, just so long as they did. If Mr. Lucas cast her as Alice, then she'd be the best damn Alice any high school had ever seen. Assuming she ever found out who Alice was.

Monday, January 20

"You got it!" Lauren screamed. "You got it! You're Alice!"

"I don't believe you," Jody said, pushing through the crowd by the bulletin board to look at the cast list. "Alice—Jody Chapman. I did! Lauren, I got the part!"

"And I'm on the prop committee," Lauren said. "That was my first choice too."

"The first rehearsal is tomorrow," Jody said. "Lauren, will you help me learn my lines?"

"If you help me find my props," Lauren replied. "Oh, Jody, this is going to be so much fun."

"It is, isn't it?" Jody said. "Fun. That's just what I'm in the mood for right now."

Tuesday, January 21

At rehearsal the next day, the cast sat around the stage and read through the first act of the play. Jody discovered that Tony, who was played by Jim Adams, was her love interest. And while Alice wasn't the biggest part in the show, and it certainly wasn't the flashiest, she was the heroine, the only sane person in a family of mad people.

Jody grinned as soon as she realized that. She'd had close to five months' training for the role, and it was about time it paid off. She loved saying Alice's lines, learning about Alice's family, worrying about Alice's future. She could hardly wait until they really started acting the play, moving around on stage, handling the props, changing into their costumes, receiving their applause. Jody didn't know who had invented the custom of school plays, but she sent a silent thank-you to whoever it was.

Wednesday, January 22

"*R*ehearsals are so much fun," Jody said to Kay, as they sat in Jody's bedroom that night. "Today we blocked Act 3—blocking is when the director shows you where to move around on stage—and we kept bumping into each other, but it didn't matter. I mean it will, if we don't learn our blocking, but Mr. Lucas says that always takes a while, and since we have a month before we actually perform the play, we should have plenty of time to learn the blocking as well as our lines. And I like Alice so much, she's such a nice person. And you know what Mr. Lucas said? After rehearsal yesterday, he walked over to me and said, 'Just be yourself, Jody, and you'll be the perfect Alice.' Isn't that great? Everybody in the play is crazy except for Alice and Tony, and he told me to just be myself. Of course he also said the same thing to Lisa Kellerman, and she plays Penny, who is the craziest person in the play, or close to it. So maybe he just says that to everybody. Or maybe he thinks Lisa is crazy. Maris certainly thinks so, and it takes one to know one."

"Are you through?" Kay asked her.

"No," Jody replied. "But I'm willing to take a break."

"Good," Kay said. "Because I really need to talk to you."

"About what?" Jody asked.

"About Michael," Kay said.

Jody shook her head. "Forget it," she said. "I'm not interested."

"But how do you know?" Kay asked. "Did it ever occur to you that maybe I had something important to say?"

"Do you know where Michael is?" Jody asked.

"No, of course not," Kay replied.

"Then I'm not interested," Jody said. "Kay, I'm having fun for the first time in months. And I refuse to listen to you or Mom or Dad or anybody about Michael, when there's nothing I can do about it. So forget it. You want to tell someone, tell someone else. I don't care who. Just leave me out of it."

"How long are you going to be like this?" Kay asked.

"At least until the play is over with," Jody informed her. "And then if I still like it, I'll stay this way forever. You might think about it too. Get involved in something. Start taking dance lessons again."

"Maybe I will," Kay said. "You sure seem happy."

"I am," Jody said. "Or at least happier. And I'll tell you the truth. It's a nice change of pace. Now, if you want to talk about anything other than Michael, I'd be happy to listen."

"Nothing right now," Kay said. "I guess I'll finish my homework."

"Good idea," Jody said. "I have a chemistry test on Friday."

"Fine," Kay said. "I hope you stay happy, Jody."

"I hope you get happy, kid," Jody replied, giving her sister a pat on the back. She didn't know how long this mood was going to last, but she was going to do everything she could to protect it for as long as she could.

Sunday, January 26

"What are you doing, Mom?" Jody asked as she made herself a sandwich for lunch.

"What does it look like I'm doing?" her mother replied. "I'm going through the classifieds for jobs."

"Jobs," Jody said, trying to keep the excitement from her voice. "You thinking about going back to work?"

"I certainly am," her mother declared. "I kept telling your father there was no point even looking during the holidays, nobody ever quits their job before Christmas, but last week I started reading through the ads, and if I don't find something really promising in today's paper, I think I'll start hitting the agencies."

"That's great, Mom," Jody said. "Dad must be real pleased."

"I'm not doing it for him," her mother said. "Or for you or Kay either. I'm doing it for myself. I can't just sit at home waiting for the door to open any longer. There's a world out there, and it's about time I plunged back into it."

"I guess it's contagious," Jody said. "Because that's exactly how I've been feeling."

Her mother looked up from the newspaper. "I've noticed," she said with a smile. "You've been a real inspiration to me, Jody. I know how much you've been suffering the past few months, and seeing the way you've been studying and trying out for the play has helped me a lot."

"I'm glad," Jody replied. "But to be perfectly honest, I was doing it for me and nobody else."

"That doesn't matter," her mother continued. "I also owe you a thank-you for putting Michael's presents away. If it had been up to me, the tree would still be there with the gifts underneath. Putting them away felt like an admission to me that

109

Michael wasn't going to be coming back. I could never have made myself do it."

"They're still waiting for him," Jody said. Kay's rock flashed through her mind and she grinned. "When he's ready for them, they'll be here."

"I'll be here too," her mother said. "Not the crazy lady I've been for the last few months either. I'm determined to be Michael's mother, just the way he'd remember me. I owe that to all of us."

"He'll be back soon," Jody said. "I feel it."

"I feel it too," her mother said. "Now scat so I can find me a job."

Tuesday, February 4

"*H*ey, Jody, wait up."

Jody turned around and saw Jim Adams chasing after her. "Sure, Jim, what's up?" she asked.

"I was wondering if we could go over lines one night this week," he said. "Tomorrow maybe, or Thursday? We could rehearse our scenes together at my house, and then go out for a pizza afterwards. Okay?"

"Sounds great," Jody said. "Tomorrow's fine."

"After rehearsal then," Jim said. "Come back home with me. I really need work on Act 1, Scene 2."

Jody grinned. "You and me both," she declared. "Tomorrow. Then the next time we do the scene at rehearsal, we'll knock 'em dead."

"My kind of co-star," Jim said. "See you tomorrow."

Wednesday, February 5

"Hi, Jody, come on in," Jim's mother said as Jim and Jody walked through the front door. "It's nice to see you again. Would you like something warm to drink?"

"Tea would be great," Jody said. "Thank you, Mrs. Adams."

"And how are your folks?" Mrs. Adams asked. "Jimmy, hang Jody's coat up nicely. I can't remember the last time I saw your mother."

"They're about the same," Jody said. "We made it through the holidays, and that was pretty rough."

"I can imagine," Mrs. Adams said. "Actually, I don't want to imagine. Jim, I made some nice apple cake for you and Jody. Go into the kitchen and bring out some slices."

"Sure, Mom," Jim said.

"And put the tea kettle on too," Mrs. Adams called to him. She turned to Jody and smiled. "Jim tells me you're wonderful in your role," she said. "I can't wait to see the show."

"It's been a lot of fun," Jody said. "Jim's very good too."

"He's certainly been working hard enough at it," his mother declared. "I've run lines with him every night for the past two weeks. He's letter-perfect in just about all his scenes."

"Is he really?" Jody said. "He's a lot further along than I am."

"He's such a perfectionist," his mother said. "About everything except hanging up coats."

"I heard that," Jim declared, walking into the living room with two pieces of cake. "Mom, how about you looking after the tea, so Jody and I can get to work."

"My pleasure," his mother said. "Jody, come more often. And call if you need anything."

"Thank you, I will," Jody promised. She looked at Jim and

111

grinned. "Your mother says you know all your lines already," she declared. "Was this a trick to get me over so I could learn mine?"

"Not quite," he said, sitting down and balancing his cake plate on his lap. "It was more like a trick so I could ask you out on a date."

"You didn't need a trick for that," Jody told him.

"I wasn't sure," Jim replied. "I know how bad things have been for you lately, and I wasn't sure if you were dating."

"Why shouldn't I be?" Jody asked. "What does one thing have to do with the other?"

"Oh, come on, Jody," Jim said. "You've been walking around under a thundercloud for months now. You haven't exactly been approachable. Even at your birthday party, I kept thinking you were going to start crying all the time. When a guy asks a girl out, he likes to think she's going to say yes, or at least smile politely when she says no. I haven't seen you smile since school started."

"I'm smiling now," Jody pointed out. "See, those are my teeth and everything."

"Does that mean you're smiling politely because you're about to say no?" Jim asked.

"I think it means I'm going to say yes if you ask me," Jody replied. "Shall we find out?"

"How about a movie Saturday night?" Jim asked. "We could double with Lauren and Todd."

"Have you spoken to Lauren and Todd about it already?" Jody asked.

Jim shrugged. "I wasn't about to take any chances," he said. "Are you free?"

"I guess I must be," Jody said. "Lauren certainly thinks I am."

"So it's a date?" Jim said.

"It's a date," Jody replied. "Assuming I know my lines by then."

"I'll coach you," Jim declared. "Come on, let's start with Act 1, Scene 2. You go first."

Saturday, February 8

"It was a funny movie, I'm not saying it wasn't," Jody declared as she sat in a booth with Jim, Lauren, and Todd. They were just finishing their sodas, but none of them was in a rush to go out into the cold February night. "But *You Can't Take It With You* is funnier."

"I'll have to take your word for it," Lauren said. "They won't let us lowly props people watch rehearsals."

"I'm not even on one of the committees," Todd said. "They won't let me walk past the auditorium after school anymore."

"You're a senior," Lauren pointed out. "Besides, why would you want to walk past the auditorium?"

"To see what's going on in there," Todd said.

"Just Mr. Lucas shouting at us," Jim told him. " 'Haven't you learned your lines yet! Don't you realize there's only two more weeks before our first performance! I'm not going to be the one making a fool of myself on stage! It's your funeral, not mine!' "

"He's never said anything about funerals," Jody declared. "The rest is pretty accurate though."

"I know what it was," Jim said. "He said the critics would bury us."

"Is it that bad?" Lauren asked. "I'd hate to think all my beautiful props are going to waste."

"I think we're great," Jody declared. "Of course Jim and I are the best, but then everyone else is working on coming up to our high standards."

"In two or three years' time, they might even have a shot at it," Jim said. "In the meantime, watch for Tony and Alice, the two best young lovers in the history of theater."

"It's an honor to be seated in the same booth with you,"

113

Todd declared. "To think you took pity on a humble senior and agreed to let him chauffeur you all over town on a freezing cold night like tonight."

"The bigger they are, the nicer they are," Lauren said. "Look how they're continuing to talk to me, lowly props person."

"I'm getting a little worried about all those lowly props," Jim said to Jody. "Do you think Lauren's going to give us miniature everythings, and we'll have to use magnifying glasses to find them?"

"No, I think she's the lowly one," Jody replied. "Lauren, I promise you, I'll lead the cast in a standing ovation for your properties."

"It's the least you could do," Lauren replied. "Todd, what time is it?"

"Eleven-fifteen," he said, checking his watch.

"Whoops," Lauren said. "I think we'd better get going. I'm due home sometime before twelve."

"There's still time before twelve," Todd said. "There's still lots of time before twelve."

"The 'sometime before twelve' I'm expected home is eleven-thirty," Lauren said. "With a ten-minute leeway. Sorry."

"I should be getting home, too," Jody said, getting up. Jim did also, and helped her on with her coat.

"I'll drop you off first," Todd said to Jody. "You're right on the way."

"And in the way," Jody said. "Fine."

They ran to the car, watching their breath waft up. The stars shone clearly down to earth, and Jody wondered, as she always did, if Michael was someplace looking at the same stars.

"Beautiful night," Jim said as they climbed into the backseat.

"If it's so beautiful, you can walk home," Todd said.

"Miserable night," Jim said. "Worst I've seen in a long time."

Everyone laughed. Todd got the car started and drove the city streets carefully until he reached Jody's house.

"I'll walk you to your door," Jim said, and he and Jody got out of the car together. They held hands as they walked up the sidewalk, and then at the front door, they kissed goodnight.

"This was fun," Jody said. "Thanks, Jim."

"Let's do it again, okay?" Jim said.

"Sounds good to me," Jody said, giving him another quick kiss. Todd honked the car horn to guarantee it wouldn't be a lengthy farewell. "See you Monday," Jody called out to Jim as he walked away.

"Work on your lines," Jim called back to her.

Jody unlocked the door and walked into her comfortably warm house. Her parents were still up, sitting in the living room, watching TV.

"Did you have a nice time?" her mother asked, as Jody hung up her coat.

"Very nice," Jody told her. "We saw *Silk Purse*. It was funny."

"We should go to the movies sometime," Jody's father said. "What do you say, Linda?"

"Whenever you want," Jody's mother replied. "Just you and me?"

"Just you and me," he said. "Dinner first, and a movie. The kids can fend for themselves one evening."

"We'd be happy to fend, Dad," Jody said. "I think it sounds like a great idea."

"A date," Jody's mother said. "Be still, my heart."

"Dutch," Jody's father said.

"You little cheapskate!" Jody's mother cried. "Tell you what. You treat for dinner, I'll pay for the movie."

"Burger Bliss it is, then," Jody's father said.

"Burger Bliss, my eye!" Jody's mother said.

"You two can work out these details without me," Jody said. "I'm going to bed."

"Sleep well, dear," her mother said. "Burger Bliss! I want a full five-course dinner, Tom. French preferably, or at least Japanese."

"You've never had one of Burger Bliss's Frenchburgers?" Jody's father said. Jody giggled as she walked upstairs. She couldn't remember the last time she'd heard so much laughter in one night. She was tempted to get out her cassette recorder and record the sounds of all the laughter, so when the time came when she forgot what it sounded like, she'd be able to listen to it and remember.

Friday, February 21

"I don't believe this," Jody whispered backstage, as they stood around waiting for the curtain to go up. "I don't remember any of my lines!"

"That's amazing," Jim said. "Because the only lines I *do* remember are yours."

"You do my part then," Jody said. "And I'll stand on stage and mouth the words."

"I always suspected you were a dummy," Jim said, kissing her lightly. "Is it bad luck to kiss backstage?"

"It doesn't matter," Jody groaned. "Jim, I think I'm going to die."

"Great," Jim said. "They'll call me the Killer Kisser in the tabloids. There goes any chance at Ivy League."

"What's my cue?" Jody asked. "If you'd just tell me my cue, then maybe I'd remember all my lines."

"How should I know your cue?" Jim asked. "I don't even know my own."

"It's too late now," Jody moaned. "They're raising the curtain."

"Break a leg," Jim whispered to her.

"You too," Jody whispered back, and positioned herself for her first entrance.

And as soon as she heard her cue line, she knew exactly what to do, where to move, and what to say. She walked into the living room set, kissed all the cast members as though they were a family, and listened as her first lines came out of her mouth just the way they had in rehearsal every day that week. In a moment, she realized people in the audience were actually laughing, and in another moment, she realized they were laughing at what she was saying.

The warmth of their laughter enveloped her, and she felt more alive than she ever had before. It seemed to affect the entire cast. Lines they had consistently flubbed now came naturally to them. Dialogue that had sounded dead every time they'd delivered it was now funny and lively and instantly responded to. The play was funny and the cast was great, and Jody loved being Alice, loved knowing that the audience was rooting for her to work things out with Tony, loved the sensation of being something more than who she was, loved the sound of the laughter from the darkened auditorium.

They performed the play in record time—nothing dragged, no lines were dropped. The cast was flushed with excitement as the audience demanded curtain call after curtain call. Finally the curtain went down, the clapping stopped, and the cast was left to hug and kiss and congratulate themselves.

"Remember, cast, same time tomorrow," Mr. Lucas said. "And no partying until the cast party tomorrow night."

"Right, Mr. Lucas," they all said, but Jody didn't care about parties. She knew she would never feel better than she did just then, no matter how many parties she attended or how many plays she performed in. That night, that performance, that moment, was the best, and nothing could ever top the feeling.

SEARCHING

Friday, March 28

*T*hey were sitting at the dinner table when the telephone rang. "I'll get it," Jody said, thinking it might be Jim calling about a change of plans for Saturday night. "Hello," she said.

"Hello, Jody?" the voice said back at her. "This is Officer Dino."

"Officer Dino," Jody said. "Do you want to talk to my parents?"

"Yes, please," he said, and Jody handed the phone over to her father. Her mother took the extension phone in the living room.

"Officer Dino?" Kay said to Jody as she sat back at the table. "What does he want?"

"I don't know," Jody whispered.

"Yes, sir," Jody's father said. "Oh, God, no."

"They've found Michael," Kay said. "He's dead."

"Stop it," Jody whispered angrily.

"Yes, I understand," her father said. "All right. Yes, I'll come right over. Yes. No, Linda, there's no reason for both of us to go. You'll make the travel arrangements? Thank you, Officer. Right, right away. Thank you." He hung up the phone and sank back into his chair.

Jody's mother walked back in and started crying. "Told you," Kay said to Jody.

"They don't know for sure," Jody's father said. "The police in Ohio have found a body of a young boy. It could be Michael, but they don't know. I'm flying out to Cleveland to see."

"Oh, God," Jody said. "How long . . ."

"They think he's been dead a week, maybe less," her father replied. "I'm sure it isn't Michael, but he's the right height and

121

same general appearance. Or so they think. It's just a formality, really. I'll fly out there, look at him, and if it isn't Michael, I'll be back tomorrow afternoon."

"What if it is Michael?" Kay asked.

"I'm sure it isn't," her father replied. "But you're all going to have to be very strong while you're waiting to hear from me. You too, Kay. There's no point falling to pieces when it probably isn't Michael anyway. And there's certainly no point in calling my parents. If it is . . . if there's anything they have to be told, there's plenty of time to tell them. Why should they worry needlessly?"

"I'm going with you," Jody's mother said.

"Linda, no," Jody's father said. "You stay here with the girls. I'll call the minute I know something."

"I'm going with you," she said. "I'm his mother, Tom. I belong there."

"We don't even know that it is Michael," Jody's father said. "Stay here, Linda. If it is Michael, and they want you to fly out, you can be there in a few hours."

"Was he murdered?" Kay asked.

"He was shot," her mother replied. "I'm going upstairs to pack our overnight bags. Jody, you'll watch out for Kay, won't you?"

"Sure, Mom," Jody said.

"There's no reason for you to go," Jody's father said. "Linda, listen."

"I will not," she said. "I'm not going to stand here fighting about this, Tom, when our son could be lying in a morgue someplace waiting for us to take him home. Jody, we'll call the minute we know anything. I don't want you leaving the house until we get back, and don't answer the phone or the door either. I'll ring once, then hang up and ring again, so you'll know it's us. If it is Michael, reporters will be calling, and I don't want you to talk with them. Do you understand me?"

"Sure, Mom," Jody said.

"Good," she said. "Tom, call Rob and tell him where we're going. I want him over here if it is Michael to wait with the girls until we get back."

"Right," Jody's father said.

"I wonder who killed him," Kay said. "Probably a sex murderer."

"Kay, stop it!" Jody said. "Dad, did Officer Dino say anything else?"

"Not now, honey," her father said, dialing his brother's phone number.

Jody looked at him and began to shake. Was it possible that it was Michael, that after seven months, they had finally found him? And if it was Michael, then would they ever learn how he had lived all those months away from home, and who his murderer was? Did he die alone in some strange town in Ohio? Were his last thoughts of his family?

"I hope it's him," Kay whispered. "I hope it's really him."

"Oh, stop it," Jody said, but the emotion was drained out of her voice. She felt nothing anymore, and knew she wouldn't until she heard from her parents about the dead boy they'd been called to claim.

Saturday, March 29

"Do you think they're there yet?" Kay asked Jody a little after one that morning.

"I guess so," Jody said. "Dad said they were flying into Cleveland, and a policeman would meet them there and drive them to Oak Glen. He said it was about fifty miles outside of Cleveland, so that should take another hour after the plane lands. They're probably there, or on their way by now."

"If it's Michael, will we have a funeral?" Kay asked.

"Of course we will," Jody said.

"Good," Kay said. "I want everybody to know he's dead already."

"I hate it when you talk like that," Jody said. "Why don't you go to sleep?"

123

"Yeah, sure," Kay said. "Jody, admit it. Don't you want it to be Michael too? Just so we'll know. Wouldn't it be better to know than to just keep on waiting all the time?"

"I don't want Michael to be dead," Jody declared. "That's all I know."

"And what if it isn't Michael?" Kay said. "Mom and Dad could be getting phone calls like this for the rest of our lives. When they die, we could get the calls. We could be grown-ups, and have jobs and boyfriends and still get calls asking us to identify somebody's body. It's going to be a lot easier if this one is Michael."

"When did you turn nasty?" Jody asked. "You never used to be nasty."

"On my birthday," Kay replied. "You know it. You just expected it to wear off and it never did."

"Are there any cookies left?" Jody asked.

"We ate them all hours ago," Kay replied. "And we finished the potato chips too and the pretzels."

"There'd better be something," Jody said, walking to the kitchen to check it out. There was nothing, at least nothing that presented itself in an easy-to-open package. "There's some brown sugar," she said. "I'm going to take a hunk of brown sugar. You want some, Kay?"

"I'm not that desperate," Kay replied.

"Well, I am," Jody said, breaking herself off a piece and carrying it back into the living room. She let the lump of sugar dissolve in her mouth and felt a little bit better.

"What if Mom forgets the signal?" Kay asked. "If it is Michael, she might be too upset to remember it."

"Then we'll answer the phone anyway," Jody said. "If it's a reporter, we'll just hang up."

"I bet if it is Michael, they'll call Rob first," Kay said. "And he'll come over and tell us in person."

"Maybe," Jody said. "That sounds like something they might do."

"I don't care," Kay said. "I don't care if the reporters are the ones to tell us. I don't care if I have to find out in the newspapers. I don't care if it is Michael." And she sat on the living room sofa and began to cry.

124

"Kay, it's all right," Jody said. "We'll find out soon."

"I don't care," Kay muttered. "Do you hear me? I don't care."

"I know," Jody said. "I don't care either."

"He's better off dead," Kay said. "Sometimes I wish I was dead too."

"No you don't," Jody said. "Kay, calm down. Eat some sugar."

Kay looked up at Jody and half laughed. "Sugar?" she said. "You think I'm a horse?"

Jody laughed with her. "You'd rather have some hay?" she asked, and the thought struck her as outrageously funny. She began to laugh, and soon Kay had joined her. They were laughing uncontrollably on the living room floor, clutching cushions, pounding the floor with their fists, trying to stop laughing, to start breathing, to behave sanely, when the telephone rang.

It rang once, then stopped, and rang again. The girls needed no other sound to calm down. Jody ran to the phone and picked it up.

"Jody darling, it's Mom," her mother said. "It isn't Michael."

"Thank God," Jody said. "You're sure?"

"Positive," her mother said. "And your father agrees completely. Here he is."

"Jody, it definitely isn't Michael," her father said. "There's some resemblance, I grant you. I understand why the police wanted us here for identification, but it definitely isn't Michael. His ears are too small. You know what big ears Michael has."

Jody tried to remember the size of Michael's ears and found she couldn't conjure up Michael. "I remember," she said. "He had very big ears."

"There were other differences, of course," her father said. "But your mother and I immediately noticed the ears. Anyway, we're going to spend the night here, and then we'll get the first flight back from Cleveland tomorrow. Thank God, this was just a wild goose chase."

"That's great," Jody said. "I guess I'll see you tomorrow then."

"Get a good night's sleep," her father said. "And if Kay's still up, kiss her goodnight for us."

"I will," Jody promised, and hung up.

"False alarm, huh?" Kay said.

Jody nodded.

"Shit," Kay said. "Now we'll just have to go through all this again and again and again."

Monday, March 31

"Jody, could you please tell us who the leading opponents to the League of Nations were in the Senate?" Jody's history teacher asked that morning.

"Excuse me?" Jody replied. She'd been staring out the window, watching the trees start to bud.

"I asked you who the leading opponents to the League of Nations were in the Senate," her teacher declared. "You're a smart girl, Jody. I'm sure you know the answer."

"Answer," Jody said, and began to laugh.

"Jody!" her teacher said sharply.

But it was too late. "Don't you know there aren't any answers?" Jody choked out, and laughed and laughed until the tears streamed down her face.

Tuesday, April 1

"Jody, wait up."

"Sure, Jim," Jody said. "What's up?"

"I think we need to talk," Jim said. "Do you mind?"

"Of course not," Jody said. "Walk me home, all right? I'm

making supper tonight. Now that Mom's working again, I'm back on kitchen duty." She realized she was chattering, but she didn't seem able to stop herself.

"You scared me in history class yesterday," Jim began. "You scared all of us."

"I know," Jody said. "I'm sorry. It was just the idea of supplying answers on demand." She started giggling again, and bit down on her lip to force herself to stop.

"Jody, I don't understand you anymore," Jim said. "You were hardly even there on our date Saturday night. I don't think you heard a word I said all evening. And then yesterday in history, the way you started laughing."

"Jim, it's been a hard few days," Jody said. "My parents went to look at a body on Friday. You know what that does to you?"

"No," Jim said. "I don't."

"It twists you inside," Jody replied. "It twists you until you aren't really human anymore. It makes you pray for things that are horrible, and then pray for forgiveness for your prayers. It makes you hate the people you love. It makes you . . ." She stopped for a moment, and looked at Jim. His seventeenth birthday was a month away, and he looked as though he hadn't started shaving yet. "You don't understand, do you?" she said.

"No," Jim said. "I don't. I know your family is going through a rough time, but I thought you'd come out of it. When we were working on the play, you seemed like your old self again. And now you seem to have lost that."

"The play was a distraction," Jody said. "A vacation. What you see now is who I really am."

"I can't handle it," Jim said. "I'm really sorry, Jody. I like you a lot. But I can't handle it when you're a thousand miles away, when you look at me like you're a hundred years old, when you start laughing hysterically in history class. It scares me, and I don't want to see you anymore."

"You have to see me," Jody pointed out. "We're in a half dozen classes together."

"I mean date you," he replied. "I don't think we should keep on seeing each other outside of school. You need someone who's smarter than me, or at least older."

127

"That isn't it," Jody said. "You need someone who's younger than me, or at least more normal."

"I'm really sorry," Jim said. "I am, Jody. For you and for your family. I hope you won't get too mad at me."

Jody smiled ruefully. "You're the least of it, Jim," she declared. "I'm so angry inside, there isn't room for me to get mad at you."

"Maybe he'll come home," Jim said. "There is still hope."

"I know," Jody said. "That's the thing I'm angriest about."

Wednesday, April 2

"So he dumped you," Maris said at lunch the next day. "Well, what did you expect?"

"I didn't expect anything," Jody replied, biting into her tuna sandwich.

"I'm disappointed in him," Lauren declared. "Jim's always liked you so much. And he's really a very nice boy."

"Nice boys are the ones you have to watch out for," Maris said. "They're so full of themselves, they're completely dishonest. Give me a man who's wild and mean. At least there you know where you stand."

"I thought you stopped seeing whatshisname," Jody said. "Brute."

"Not Brute," Maris said. "Knute. He was Swedish, I think, not that he ever talked enough for me to be sure. And yes, I have stopped seeing him."

"Not wild enough for you, I suppose," Lauren said. "Who are you seeing now? Some Hell's Angel?"

"His name is Dirk," Maris replied.

"Dirk the Jerk," Lauren said.

"Just 'cause you're scared of men is no reason to tease me," Maris said. "Dirk's gorgeous. He's twenty-three years old and he owns his own motorcycle and a car, and my mother is crazy with jealousy that he prefers me."

"Maris," Jody said, but then she stopped.

"Go on," Maris said. "Say what's on your mind."

"Nothing," Jody said.

"I think what Jody wants to say is you're too young to be dating twenty-three-year-olds," Lauren declared. "And your mother is too old. Right, Jody?"

"Is that what you think, Jody?" Maris asked.

Jody looked at her two best friends. "Jim split up with me because he thinks I'm crazy," she said. "What difference does it make what I think about Maris and her mother?"

"It makes a difference to me," Maris said. "We've been best friends practically all our lives, Jody. We've been through everything together. I want to know what you think and not just what Miss Goody Two Shoes says you think."

"I think you're going to do whatever you want no matter what I think," Jody replied. "First you were wild about Marco, but then you decided he bored you. Then Knute showed up and you were in love, until you said his jealousy was driving you crazy. So you dumped Knute and now it's Dirk, and he's chasing after you and your mother is chasing after him, and after Dirk it'll just be somebody else who's older and meaner and more jealous, and then somebody after that, and I don't care. I'm sorry, Maris, but I really don't."

"I hope you were listening to that, Maris," Lauren said. "Jody said something very important to you."

"I'm not much happier with you, Lauren," Jody said. "You always act like you know what's best for everybody. Well, you don't. If Maris wants to wreck her life, that's her business, not yours."

"I know you're upset because Jim dumped you," Lauren said. "So I won't pay any attention to what you just said."

Maris laughed. "I'm supposed to pay attention when Jody rakes me over the coals," she said. "But when she offers just a little bit of well-founded criticism to you, it doesn't count because she's upset."

"I don't like either of you anymore," Jody declared. "I know I used to, and neither of you has changed all that much, so it must be me, but I really don't like you."

"You don't like anybody right now," Lauren said. "It's because of Michael. You'll get over it."

"That's what you don't understand," Jody said. "I'm never going to get over it. The way I am right now is the way I'm always going to be." She sighed and took another bite of her sandwich.

"I don't feel very well," Lauren said, getting up. "If you'll both excuse me, I think I'll sit somewhere else."

"Be my guest," Maris said.

Lauren took her tray and her books and walked across the cafeteria. Jody continued to eat her sandwich.

"She'll be back, you know," Maris said. "And I'm not even leaving. Like it or not, you're stuck with us."

"Fine," Jody said. "I really don't care."

"Great," Maris said. "Don't care. But let me tell you something, I liked you a lot more when you did."

Jody looked down at her tray.

"You're not the only one who's lost your family," Maris said. "I lost them too. Your family saved me so many times, I lost count. Even last summer, when things were bad with your parents, I always knew I could go to your house, and there'd be some kind of peace for me. Someplace where I wouldn't have to deal with my mother, where I could have a real dinner with real conversation, and I always felt welcome there. Maybe I wasn't, maybe it was all a big act, but it didn't matter. It was more home to me than my home's been in years, and now there's no place for me."

"I'm sorry," Jody said. "We can't even help each other at home anymore. We're the walking dead. It's all we can do to get up in the morning, to eat our meals, to sleep at night. There's nothing left for anyone else. My mother can't help my father, I can't help Kay. You can't possibly expect us to help you."

"I don't expect anything," Maris said. "I just wanted you to know you're not the only one in pain around here."

"I know," Jody said. "Maris, I wish things were different. I'd give anything to have things the way they were. But there's no going back."

"There never is," Maris said. "Oh, dammit, I'm going to start crying."

"Don't," Jody said. "Because if you do, I will too."

"Sorry," Maris said, beginning to sob.

David Templeton, Jody said to herself, but it wasn't enough. She could feel the tears pouring down her cheeks.

"The two of you are helpless," Lauren said, plopping her tray down on the table. "Absolutely helpless. Crying in the cafeteria like two babies. What am I going to do with you?"

"You can start by passing the tissues," Maris said, and as Lauren dug them out of her pocketbook, Jody felt the tears subside and the first swell of laughter rising from deep within her.

Thursday, April 24

"*T*hank you for seeing me," John Grainger said, as he sat in the living room for the first time in months. Baron rested on Jody's lap, and she took comfort from the feel of his furry body on hers. Kay sat beside her on the sofa, and Jody was aware of just how young and small she still was.

"You don't have anything to tell us, do you?" Jody's mother asked.

"I'm afraid not," Mr. Grainger replied. "Mr. and Mrs. Chapman, I told you last December that the odds were I wouldn't be able to help you. I have looked and looked and looked, traced every lead, every possibility, checked things out that held even the remotest flicker of hope, but there's nothing. Absolutely nothing. I'm very sorry, but I just can't help you."

"Have you told my parents?" Jody's father asked.

"I wrote to them officially resigning from the case today," Mr. Grainger replied. "There's no point in their paying me any longer."

"So you're just quitting," Jody's mother said. "Like that."

"If I thought there was any chance I might be able to find

out what's happened to Michael, I'd stay on, Mrs. Chapman," Mr. Grainger said. "I don't like failing, and a case like this you get involved with. You get to care about the people. But let me be honest with you. The longer you go without hearing from Michael, the more likely it is your son is dead. And if that is the case, the police are a lot more likely to find him than I am."

"I don't believe he's dead!" Jody's mother cried. "I don't care what anybody says. I'll never believe he's dead, never!" She rose from her chair and ran from the room upstairs.

"I'm sorry," Jody's father said. "We've suspected for a long time that you weren't going to find out anything, but hearing it from you, well, it's a shock anyway."

"Of course I'll keep my ears out," Mr. Grainger declared. "I have connections, I might luck onto some information. And I'm very sorry it had to end this way. I wanted to bring Michael home to you. I had dreams of doing it."

"We've all had dreams," Jody's father replied. "Maybe now is the time for us to stop dreaming, and face the facts we've all spent months avoiding."

Monday, April 28

"They killed him," Jody's father said. "The police killed him."

Jody looked up from her chemistry homework. She and her father were the only two people in the living room, but she knew his remarks weren't directed at her. "What do you mean?" she asked anyway. "How did the police kill him?"

"All those hours they wasted claiming we shouldn't be worrying," her father replied. "All those precious hours when Michael was missing and Officer Dino was ranting about runaways. If we just had those hours back with the full police force out there searching for him, then Michael would be home today.

If he's dead, it's because of those hours, because the police killed him with their smug, self-righteous negligence."

"We don't know that he's dead," Jody pointed out, closing her chemistry book. "We don't know that he was abducted. For all we know, Officer Dino was right, and Michael did run away."

"I don't believe that, any more than you do," her father said.

"I don't believe anything anymore," Jody said. "I gave up believing a long time ago."

"If we do find him, and he is dead, I swear I'll kill Dino," her father said. "I'll strangle him if I have to, break his rotten neck with my own two hands."

"Fine, Dad," Jody said, opening her chemistry book again. "Give me a call and I'll find you a lawyer."

"They killed him," her father said. "Those rotten stupid cops killed my son."

But Jody was no longer listening.

Monday, May 12

"Jody," Lauren said, as Jody started walking up the stairs to the school building. "Jody, I don't believe that ad."

"What ad?" Jody asked. "What are you talking about?"

"The ad in the *Gazette,*" Lauren replied. "Didn't you see it this morning?"

"We don't get the *Gazette* anymore," Jody said. "Mom says it's too depressing."

"Well, I clipped it out," Lauren said. "When did your parents decide to put it in?"

Jody looked at the torn sheet from the newspaper. Underneath an ad for the local shoe outlet was a small boxed ad that read: "Michael Chapman, please call home. Your family loves and misses you. Tom, Linda, Jody, and Kay."

"Oh Jesus," Jody said. "My parents never put that in."

"They must have," Lauren said. "Who else would have?"

133

"I don't know," Jody said. "But not them. Dad thinks Michael is dead these days, and Mom has never accepted the possibility that he ran away. Besides, what's the point of advertising locally? If Michael did run away, he'd hardly be reading the *Gazette*."

"You think Kay did it?" Lauren asked.

"That's as good a guess as any," Jody replied. "I'll ask her after school today."

Any illusions Jody had that the school day would be an easy one vanished as soon as she walked in. Kids all around her were buzzing over the ad and she was approached before, during, and after all her classes about it.

"I don't know who put it in," she said patiently again and again and again. "It doesn't make any sense to me. We all think Michael was abducted. None of us thinks he ran away."

It didn't seem to matter what she told anybody though. Even the teachers asked her about the ad. And the rumors started growing too, that there had been word from Michael on his birthday, at Christmas, as recently as two weeks before. The questions grew nastier as the day progressed. Was it true the family had known all along where Michael was but hadn't wanted to admit to anyone that he was a prostitute, working the streets of New York? Was it true Jody's mother had had a breakdown in February and had been institutionalized ever since? Was it true Michael had run away because his uncle had seduced him, his father had beaten him, his mother had discovered that he was addicted to cocaine? What was the truth?

"There is no truth," Jody muttered over and over again, but the answer satisfied nobody. There had to be a truth, she was told. Maybe she didn't want to admit it, but there had to be a secret truth.

The secret truth, Jody realized by the end of the school day, was that she was going to kill her kid sister and really put her family on the map. She was even willing to endure the headlines for the pleasure it would give her to feel Kay's neck snap under her powerful grip. Jody ran through the crowd of questioners after school that day, people who had been politely or not so politely leaving her alone for months, but who now felt free to ask her anything because the Chapman name was in the paper again, ran through the crowd of people who regarded themselves as her friends, her teachers, ran away from the school, away from the crowd, and back to her home, where she could be the inquisitor for a change.

"Kay, where are you?" she screamed as she opened the door. "Kay, you'd better be here!"

"I'm in the kitchen," Kay said. "What are you so mad about?"

"Mad?" Jody shouted. "Mad? What am I so mad about?"

"You look like you're having a fit," Kay said. "Your face is all red, Jody. Sit down. Maybe you should drink some water."

"Maybe I should strangle you first," Jody said. "Why did you put the ad in, Kay?"

"What makes you so sure I was the one who put it in?" Kay replied.

"Because Mom and Dad never would have," Jody said. "Only you would be that stupid."

"There was nothing stupid about it," Kay said, and for the first time in months Jody saw a glimmer of just how young Kay really was. "I knew Michael wouldn't read it in the *Gazette*. I know he isn't anywhere near here."

"Then why put it in?" Jody asked, sitting down at the kitchen table. "What's the point?"

"We need the publicity," Kay said. "Nobody looks at the posters anymore. We can put them in stores from now until doomsday saying 'Still Missing' and 'Not Yet Found,' but nobody's going to look anymore. I figured if I put the ad in, maybe some reporter somewhere would think it was worth an article, you know, 'Kid sister uses all her money in last-ditch attempt to locate missing brother.' And maybe lots of newspapers would pick up the article, or even TV, and then Michael might hear about it and if he did run away, he'd realize we all do love him. And even if he didn't run away, if someone is holding him prisoner somewhere, he'd know we still love him, and maybe that would give him the strength to escape."

"Oh, Lord," Jody said, sitting back in her chair.

"Someone had to do something," Kay said. "We can't just forget about Michael."

"We're not going to forget," Jody said. "Where did you get the money? Ads that big must cost a lot."

"I returned all my Christmas presents and got money for them," Kay said. "And I told Granny that Mom had stopped giving me an allowance because she was mad at me for wanting

135

to spend Christmas with her, so Gran's been sending me money every week, and I've been saving the allowance Mom has been giving me, and I stole the rest from Mom and Dad mostly. A little from you. Some from people in school. I just waited to see if Mr. Grainger would come through. I've been planning this for months."

"I can see," Jody said. "I wish you'd consulted me first though."

"I tried to," Kay said. "A long time ago. But you said you didn't want to talk about Michael anymore. And I figured you meant it."

"You told me you wished he was dead," Jody replied. "How could I talk to you?"

"I still wish he was dead," Kay said. "I wish the police would find him and send him back to us and we could have a big funeral and invite the world, and then we could wear black for a while and be done with it. But you can't know that he's dead, and as long as you can't, then I figured we'd better keep trying to find him. So I put the ad in. Do you think Mom and Dad are going to be mad?"

"You know they are," Jody said.

"I'll go live with Gran," Kay said. "She gives me more allowance than Mom does anyway."

Jody looked at her sister. "I'll talk to Mom and Dad," she said. "And try to cool them down. Why don't you stay at a friend's house until I give you the all-clear signal?"

"I don't have any friends," Kay said. "Nobody's liked me in months."

"There are reasons for that," Jody replied. "Go over to Lauren's, then."

"Oh, Jody, do I have to?" Kay asked. "Can't I stay with Maris instead?"

"Absolutely not," Jody said. "She'd probably arrange a double date with Knute and Dirk. Lauren's much safer. You go over there, and I'll call you after I've explained the situation to Mom and Dad."

Kay sat quietly for a moment, thinking about it. "No," she said at last. "I did what I thought was right. I'd better stay here and tell them why."

"Kay, it isn't necessary," Jody said. "And it isn't smart. You saw how angry I was. Mom's going to be a hundred times worse."

"I don't care," Kay said. "I did what was right. Besides, if I go over to Lauren's, all I'll get is lectures from her, and then I'll come home and get lectures from Mom and Dad anyway. I might as well skip the middleman."

"Then at least go up to your room," Jody said. "There's no reason for you to confront Mom directly."

But it was too late. Even as Jody was saying the words, she could hear her mother driving her car down the driveway.

"Wish me luck," Kay whispered, and Jody, despite herself, crossed her fingers.

Jody's mother unlocked the kitchen door and stormed in. "You idiot!" she screamed at Kay, and without taking a breath, ran over to her and slapped her hard across her face. "You stupid idiot!" And she slapped her again.

"Mom," Jody said in horror. Kay sat still, her mouth hanging open, too paralyzed to cry.

"Isn't my life hell enough?" her mother said. "Don't I have enough to endure, never knowing, never being able to think of anything else but my son? I need this from you? I need this stupid, deceitful treachery?" She raised her hand again to strike Kay, but Jody got up, and pulled her mother back.

"Stop it," Jody said. "Mom, stop it right now."

"Stay out of this, Jody," her mother said. "This is between your sister and me. Your sister, who has no love for anybody in this family anymore. Your sister, who I'm ashamed to call my daughter."

"Mommy," Kay whimpered, beginning to cry.

"She did it for a reason," Jody said. "Mom, she might have been wrong, but she did it because she loves Michael, because she loves all of us."

"The hell she did," her mother said. "Maybe she has you fooled, but not me. Not anymore. This time, you've gone too far, Kay. This time you've taken your nasty little jealousies a step too far."

"Stop it, Mom," Jody said. "Kay, go upstairs."

"No, Kay, stay right where you are," her mother said. "You

137

might as well hear this now. Your father and I had a half a dozen conversations today at work, when we had the chance to call each other, in between all the questions, the endless questions everyone kept asking us, and we've decided that we don't want you living with us anymore."

"What?" Jody said. Kay was crying too hard to speak.

"You'll finish out the school year," her mother said. "And then you'll spend the summer with your grandparents, assuming they're willing to have you."

"That's not a bad idea," Jody said. "It'll give all of us a chance to calm down."

"And then in the fall, we're sending you to boarding school," her mother continued. "You can come home for holidays, but that's it. We don't care how many homesick phone calls you make, how hard you beg us to let you back home, you're staying in school. I can't live under the same roof with you anymore. The very sight of you sickens me. And I want you to know, Jody, that the money we're going to be spending on boarding school is coming from your college fund. Kay's ruining your life just the same as she's ruining ours."

"Mom," Jody said. "All she did was try to help."

"Kay isn't interested in helping," her mother said. "Don't you think I hear her prayers every night, 'Oh, God, let Michael be dead. Oh, God, let them find his body'? Sometimes I think Kay killed him, that Michael is dead because Kay killed him with her thoughts. Michael, my only son. And I want you to know, Kay, if we do find out Michael is dead, I will never speak to you again. I don't care how old you'll live to be, I will never speak to you or see you again, because I'll know you killed him as surely as if you'd pulled the trigger on the gun. You're sick, Kay, sick and warped and evil, and it sickens me to think I ever loved you, that Michael ever loved you. I just hope we can find a school somewhere whose standards are so low they'll be willing to take you."

"I'm going," Kay said, getting up. "I'll go right now if I make you that sick."

"You're not leaving this house," her mother said. "Go to your room and stay there. I won't have you running away, telling everybody what a cruel and unloving mother you have. I'm a thousand times better than you deserve. Go to your room and stay there until I tell you you can come out. And don't even think about calling your precious grandmother to see if she'll help you. Your father already called her, and she knows just how evil you are."

"I'm not the one who's evil," Kay said, wiping the tears off her cheeks. "You are. You all are."

"Get out," her mother said. "Go to your room right now."

"I'm going with her," Jody said.

"Fine," her mother said. "But don't think you're going to be able to change her with any kind little words."

Jody stared at her mother, then put her arm around Kay's trembling shoulders. The girls walked out of the kitchen and up to Kay's bedroom. Jody expected Kay to fling herself on her bed and weep for hours, but instead Kay blew her nose and sat down on the chair by her desk.

"I'm sorry about the college fund," Kay said, and swallowed hard. She closed her eyes for a moment, and Jody saw her willing her tears away. "I am sorry about that, Jody."

"I know," Jody said. "Besides, it doesn't matter. They'll change their minds. Mom's furious now, but she'll calm down, and Dad probably isn't as mad as she is anyway."

"I want to go away though," Kay said. "I don't want to be a part of this family anymore. Not that it's really a family."

"Kay, you don't mean that," Jody said. "No more than Mom means what she was saying."

Kay shook her head. "You don't understand," she said. "You never really have. When Mom and Dad were talking about getting a divorce last summer, you kept acting as though it was just a phase they were going through. When Mom went crazy last fall, you acted like she was behaving perfectly normally."

"She was," Jody said. "It was a crazy situation, so crazy behavior was normal."

Kay shuddered. Jody could see the price she was paying to stay in control.

"She's still crazy, Jody," Kay said. "She has to hate someone because of what's happened, and I'm the easiest one to hate so she hates me. It's been like that for months now. I do pray that Michael is dead, she wasn't lying, but sometimes I pray it so

139

she'll hate someone else—whoever murdered Michael, or even Michael himself for being dead, just as long as she stops hating me. It's not my fault I'm still here. I don't ask her to listen at my door. I hate her too, Jody, but I hate her for hating me. That's all. If she ever stopped hating me, then I'd stop hating her, but she won't stop until we find out what happened to Michael."

"Kay, Mom isn't an easy person under the best of circumstances," Jody said. "We've talked about that. I had terrible fights with her when I was your age."

"Never this terrible," Kay said.

"No," Jody said. "Never this terrible."

"It's okay," Kay said, biting down on her lip. "I mean I hurt all over and I'm so scared, but it's okay. I want to go away to school. I want a fresh chance. I want to go someplace where everything doesn't revolve around Michael. I don't want her to be my mother any more than she wants me to be her daughter."

"Kay, no," Jody said, but Kay had dissolved into tears. She buried her head on her desk, and began weeping with a depth of pain that startled even Jody, who thought she had seen all there was of pain in this world.

Tuesday, May 13

*I*t was raining the next morning, but Kay decided to walk to school anyway, and left early, after asking permission to borrow an umbrella. Those were the only words she spoke that morning.

Jody's father left the kitchen to get his raincoat from the hall closet, and Jody followed him.

"I can't believe you're doing this to Kay," she said to him. "Sending her away."

"It's between your mother and Kay," her father replied. "This house has become a battleground, and it's driving your mother crazy. She says the only solution is to put some distance between them, and I have to go along with what she says."

"No, you don't," Jody whispered angrily. "If you don't think it's right for Kay, then do something about it."

"Jody, stop," her father pleaded. "None of this . . . Jody, please. Goddammit, I lost a son too." His face crumpled and for a moment he sobbed. Then he pulled himself together, got his coat and briefcase, took a deep breath, kissed Jody on her cheek, and said, "It'll work out. Just give it some time," and left by the front door.

Jody watched as he walked out the door and found she could no longer be sure he would ever walk back in. She was sure of nothing, she realized, and then she realized she no longer even cared. "I wonder when I died," she murmured to herself, but knowing there would be no answer, she got her raincoat and proceeded to leave the house.

Saturday, June 21

"Dad'll be here in a minute," Jody said to Kay as they stood in line to check her in at the airport. "He'll park the car and come right in. We'll wait with you until they announce your flight."

"It's okay, Jody," Kay replied. "I know he'll be here. Relax."

"I wish I could," Jody said. "You have everything?"

"I have what I need," Kay said. "Granny'll want to take me shopping the minute I get off the plane anyway. You know how she loves to spend money on me."

"She'll spoil you rotten," Jody said. "You'll have a great summer. Granny'll feed you, but you'll burn it all off swimming every day."

"It's a good thing I like to swim," Kay said. "And eat." She smiled at her sister.

Jody hugged Kay and broke off the embrace only because the line had shuffled ahead a space. "You'll be okay?" she said. "You know we all love you."

Kay smiled.

"She loves you too," Jody said, wishing she could put more conviction in her voice.

"I don't want to talk about her," Kay said. "Jody, take care of Dad. He's really looking awful."

"He doesn't want you to go," Jody replied.

"He has a funny way of showing it," Kay said. "Jody, if it gets too bad for you, come down too. There's room for both of us, Granny told me. She hates Mom, she doesn't want either of us anywhere near her. She said they'd find me a boarding school in Florida, so I could visit them at holidays, and she said she and Granddad would pay for it if I agreed never to see Mom again. That way they won't have to touch your college fund."

"Kay, please," Jody said. "This business with Mom will work itself out. Stay out of it with Granny. Don't play them against each other."

"Why not?" Kay asked. "A girl's got to have some fun." The line inched forward, and Kay and Jody kept pace with it.

"I don't want to lose you," Jody said.

"You won't," Kay said. "At least not the same way we lost Michael. You'll hear from me, you'll see me when you come down to visit Granny and Granddad. Maybe you could go to college in Florida, and then we could see each other a lot."

"You'll be back here next fall," Jody said. "I promise. You'll be living at home and going to school here just the way you should."

"I sure hope not," Kay declared. "Jody, if you do anything to pressure Mom into letting me back, I'll never speak to you again. I mean it. I'm getting what I want, and she can never blame me. If you force her to invite me back, and I turn her down, then I get to be the bad guy all over again, and I won't have it. Do you hear me, Jody? I won't have it."

"Kay," Jody pleaded.

"You do what you want to save this family, but leave me out of it," Kay said. "I'm going to live in Florida and have a suntan year round and I'm never coming back here again. That's the way I want it and that's the way Mom wants it, and we're the only two who count."

"You can change your mind," Jody said. "It's all right to change your mind."

"I'm not going to," Kay said. She had made it to the front of the line, and handed her ticket over to the airline clerk. She put her two bags down, and watched as they were ticketed to Miami.

"I'm flying alone," she said to the clerk. "I'm going to visit my grandparents."

"Isn't that nice," the clerk said. "No smoking, I assume?"

"You assume correctly," Kay said with a broad smile. "And I'd like a window seat, if there are any left."

"I think we can arrange that," the clerk said, checking things out on the computer. "Here's your boarding pass, young lady. And I hope you have a nice visit with your family."

"I hope it's nice too," Kay said. "I know it'll be long." She walked away from the counter and Jody followed her.

"There's no point in your waiting," Kay told her. "I think I'm going to go to the boarding area now. You and Dad can just drive back."

"We will not," Jody said. "We're going to wait with you until the last possible minute."

"Jody, please," Kay said, and her smile and her toughness evaporated. "Go now. I don't think I'll be able to get on that plane if I know you're still here."

"Kay," Jody said, but Kay broke away from her and began running toward her gate. Jody started to follow, and then stopped. The last sight she had of her sister was a small figure, becoming smaller and smaller, running away, putting as much distance as she could between herself and her life.

Wednesday, July 30

*J*ody woke up at eleven and lingered in bed for another twenty minutes before finally acknowledging that she had to get out. She went to the bathroom and brushed her teeth, but didn't bother getting dressed before going downstairs to find something to eat. She'd slept until past twelve the day before, and had gotten up then only because the soap operas were already on. Jody had developed a taste for the soaps that summer. She liked to compare notes, their family problems against hers.

There was a message from her mother on the kitchen table. "Go to the store and pick up a dozen eggs, a quart of milk, and four hard rolls," it said. Jody yawned. It made no sense to buy four rolls when there were only three of them, but old habits died hard. They'd bought for five for months before they'd finally wised up. By September, she figured, the order would be for three of everything.

If she wanted to watch all the soaps all the way through, then she'd better get dressed and buy the groceries right away, she realized, so she went upstairs, took a quick shower, and dressed in the clothes she'd left lying on the floor the night before. Jody was developing a real fondness for being a slob. She wasn't seeing anybody, so it didn't matter what she looked like. Her parents certainly didn't notice, or if they did, they weren't saying.

Of course, they hadn't been saying much of anything since Kay left for Florida. Jody had expected things to quiet down after Kay left, but it was like living in a Trappist monastery, the conversation lately limited to *Please pass the*'s and *Thanks for the*'s. That was fine with Jody. She didn't have anything more to say to them than they had to say to her or each other. Without Kay around, there was no need to talk.

Jody walked downstairs, took the money her mother had left, opened the back door to let Baron in, then strolled toward the market. Milk, eggs, and rolls, she hummed to herself. She'd been forgetting things lately, but that was because she wasn't paying attention. She'd used all her powers of concentration to study for her finals, and once they were over with, there was no point in bothering to listen. Milk, eggs, and rolls. Eggs, milk, and rolls. Wholesome American items for a wholesome American family.

"I need four rolls," she announced as she walked into the store.

"All right, Jody," Mrs. Donahue replied, and took the rolls out of the box for her.

Jody went for the eggs next, pulled out a carton, and put it down next to the bag of rolls. She opened up the refrigerated cabinet and took out a carton of milk.

"Have you seen this child?" the milk carton had printed on its side.

Jody grinned at the question and then looked down. There was Michael staring back at her.

Jody read the description under the picture quickly to prove to herself it really was her Michael. Michael Chapman, right birth date, right height, weight, hair, and eye color. Michael with big ears. Michael, once her brother, and now just another missing kid, just another picture on the side of a milk carton.

Jody shoved the container back into the cabinet and started to shake.

"Are you all right?" Mrs. Donahue asked.

"I'm okay," Jody said, not wanting to explain. "I took the wrong kind of milk, that's all." She opened the cabinet and pulled out a different brand of milk, one that performed no public service on the sides of its container, but merely advertised its own brand of ice cream.

Jody put the milk down on the counter, handed Mrs. Donahue the money, and counted along with her as she was given her change. She took the bag of groceries with her out of the store and walked home slowly at first, and then faster and faster, running away from the waxen image of Michael, waiting to be purchased by someone who wouldn't care.

Friday, August 1

"Maris, we have to talk."

"Jody," Maris said from the other end of the phone line. "You haven't spoken to me all summer. You hardly spoke to me in the spring. Now out of nowhere you call, and you don't even say hello, just that we have to talk. This is not how you treat a friend."

"I'm sorry, Maris," Jody said. "Are you free now? I really need to talk with you."

"I gathered," Maris replied. "I spoke to Lauren earlier this week and she says you haven't called her either. What's going on? Aren't things better now that Kay's gone?"

"I need your help, Maris," Jody said. "I'd ask Lauren, but it involves lying, and I don't think she'd do that for me."

"But I would," Maris said. "Good old Maris. You can always count on her to lie. You want me to cheat and steal for you while I'm at it?"

"Maris, I have to go to New York and look for Michael," Jody said. "Now, are you going to help me or not?"

"Michael's in New York?" Maris asked. "You've heard from him?"

"We haven't heard a thing," Jody replied. "I don't know if he is in New York. But it seems to me kids who run away either go to New York or LA, and New York's a lot closer. So I thought I'd look for him there. He might be there."

"He might," Maris said. "Are you prepared for it if he isn't?"

"We can't be any worse off than we are now," Jody said. "And if I do find him, then maybe I can still save everything. I have to try, Maris. I've been giving up on everything lately. All I do is sleep."

146

"There are worse ways to spend a summer," Maris said.

"It won't be just for the summer," Jody replied. "It'd be like this for the rest of my life. I've been a zombie for months now, since before Kay left. And I can't stay this way. I have to do something, and I figure I have as good a chance of finding him as anybody else. Kids probably wouldn't talk to Mr. Grainger, because he's so old, and they certainly wouldn't talk to the police. But they might talk to me."

"And they might not," Maris pointed out. "Or you might not find the right kids to talk to."

"I have to try," Jody said. "Maris, I saw his face on a milk carton."

"Oh," Maris said. "I guess if milk cartons can look for Michael, you can too."

Jody nodded. "I don't dare tell my parents," she said. "So I need you to cover for me. I'm going to tell them we're together for a few days."

"Staying where?" Maris asked. "Your parents would never believe you'd moved in with me. No matter how bad things are in your home, they've still got to be better than living with my mother."

"I'm going to tell them your aunt and uncle invited us to their beach house," Jody said. "They'll believe that."

"It sounds great," Maris said. "Of course my aunt and uncle have refused to have anything to do with me since they met Jordon, but I don't suppose that matters."

"Jordon," Jody said, from force of habit.

"He's this great guy I've been seeing," Maris replied. "Twenty-seven, and you should see his sports car."

"As long as my parents don't know, it doesn't matter," Jody said. "It's not like they're going to go looking for me. I just need to tell them something. Is it okay with you?"

"Sure," Maris said. "I love being part of a conspiracy. How long are you going to stay in New York?"

"I don't know," Jody said. "I'm hoping I'll just find Michael, and then we'll come right home."

"But if you don't just find him, you can't stay there forever," Maris declared. "Have you given yourself a deadline?"

147

"I'll know when I get there," Jody said. "I want to go tomorrow. So I'm going to tell my parents tonight, and then tomorrow morning I want you to call and tell my parents your aunt's expecting us that afternoon. They're more likely to believe me if you call too."

"Okay," Maris said. "Then what do we do?"

"You go out with Jordon for all I care," Jody replied. "I'll walk over to the bus station and get a bus to New York."

"It's a long bus ride," Maris said.

"I'll buy some candy at the bus station," Jody said. "Maris, this is the most important thing I've ever asked you to do for me. It's probably the most important thing I've ever done. Please help."

"Sure, why not," Maris said. "Just don't turn out like Michael. Remember to come home, please."

"I will, I promise," Jody said. "And maybe I'll have Michael with me when I do."

Saturday, August 2

The minute Jody got off the bus, she realized it was a lost cause.

The Port Authority building, where the bus unloaded, was huge, jammed with people, and terrifying. And Jody knew it was just the tiniest percentage of New York. How was she supposed to find Michael, if she wasn't even sure she could find her way out of the building?

She walked around, clutching her bag to her side, looking at all the faces of all the people. They all seemed to be in a hurry, and none of them looked as though they'd have the slightest idea of how to start searching for Michael. She'd been an idiot to think she could ever do what Mr. Grainger and the police had failed at. They were experts at looking for people. All she was

was a kid, and no matter how strong an argument for going to the city that had seemed back home, it felt like a horrible, crippling handicap now that she was actually there.

The sight of a police officer panicked her, and Jody walked rapidly away from him, then shrank back, leaning against a wall, and felt her heart pounding. If she couldn't survive this chaos, how could she dream that Michael had? She would have started crying, but she was shaking too hard.

"I don't know who you are, kid, but if I were you, I'd take the next bus back home," a girl's voice said to Jody.

Jody twirled around and saw a girl standing next to her. She didn't seem much older than Jody, but she had on a lot of makeup and a very short skirt with a halter top. Jody took a deep breath and tried to smile at her benefactor.

"Whatever you've run away from, it probably isn't much worse than what you'll find here," the girl declared.

"I haven't run away," Jody said. "Honest. My name is Jody Chapman and I'm looking for my brother."

"Is he supposed to pick you up?" the girl asked. "You can get him paged if you want."

"No, it isn't like that," Jody said. "He doesn't know I've come to New York."

"This is all very mysterious, but some of us have to make a living," the girl said. "If you tell me where he lives, I'll give you directions, and then we can both get going."

"My brother is fourteen," Jody said. "His name is Michael, Michael Chapman. He's been missing for almost a year now, and I've come to New York to see if I can find him."

"You think he's living here?" the girl asked. "On the streets?"

"I don't know," Jody replied. "I just know I have to try and find him." She felt sure of that again, now that she had someone to talk to. Just the sort of person Mr. Grainger would have never been able to make contact with, the sort of person who could really help.

"Well, he won't be in Port Authority," the girl said. "Nobody stays here after the first ten minutes. The pimps grab 'em too fast. Is he pretty?"

"Michael?" Jody said. "I don't know. I never thought of

him as pretty. I have a picture." She pulled one out of her bag and showed it to the girl.

"I've never seen him," the girl said, checking the photograph out. "Of course that doesn't mean anything. New York's a big city. There are lots of kids working the streets. No way anybody could know all of them."

"Then Michael could be here," Jody said. "Even though you don't know him."

The girl looked at Jody. "You really want to find him?" she said. "It's that important to you?"

"He's my brother," Jody said.

The girl shrugged. "I was damn glad to get away from my brothers," she said. "How old did you say this Michael was?"

"Fourteen," Jody said. "He'll be fifteen in September."

"And you think he's been in New York for a year now," the girl said.

"I don't know," Jody replied. "I've come to look for him, but I don't know where he is."

"If he's been here on the streets for a year, you might not want to know him," the girl told Jody. "You might not even recognize him."

"He's my brother. I'll know him," Jody said. "Do you know any way I could find him?"

The girl led Jody out of the building. They stood on Eighth Avenue. It was almost sundown, but the heat was still oppressive and the air was heavy with humidity. Jody could feel the sweat on her forehead. She wiped it off with the back of her hand.

"I gotta go to work," the girl said. "I just went in there to pee. Look, there's a boy I know named Frankie. He's been in the city for a while, he seems to know lots of people. Maybe he knows this Michael of yours."

"Frankie," Jody said. "Where would I find him?"

"He hangs out a lot in front of the New Apollo Theater," the girl replied. "It's two blocks up on the corner. You could wait for him there."

"How will I know him?" Jody asked.

The girl sighed. "I'll walk you up there," she said. "And if he's there, I'll introduce you, and if he's not, I'll leave you there.

150

I really gotta get to work, but you're such a babe, you probably wouldn't be safe even in front of the New Apollo. Come on."

Jody followed the girl the two blocks, waiting with her at corners until the light changed. She had never seen so many people before in her life, and none of them were smiling. Several of them were dressed like the girl was, and she could see her new friend looking around, waving hello at some of the others.

"Lots of action tonight," the girl said. "Don't get involved with any of it."

"I won't," Jody said. "You're very nice. Thank you."

"Nice," the girl said with a smile. "There's a word I haven't heard in a long time."

"Where are you from?" Jody asked.

"Nowhere," the girl replied. "And I'm never going back there either."

"I know the feeling," Jody said.

"No, you don't," the girl said. "Good, you're in luck. I see Frankie out there, and he's all alone. He's the one in the Bruce Springsteen T-shirt. See him?"

Jody nodded.

"I gotta run," the girl said. "Tell Frankie Anise sent you."

"Anise?" Jody said.

"It's my name," the girl replied. "I think it's pretty. Good luck with your brother. Bye."

"Bye," Jody said, feeling very alone and very afraid. Maybe this was a setup. But if it was, she couldn't see what Anise stood to gain from it. And maybe Frankie could help her. So she kept on walking until she was standing in front of a boy in a Bruce Springsteen T-shirt. "Frankie?" she said.

"Yeah," the boy said.

"Anise said I should talk to you," Jody said.

"Anise," Frankie said. "Oh, okay. Anise. What does she want?"

"Nothing," Jody said. "She just said you might be able to help me."

Frankie looked down at Jody. "Help you how?" he asked.

"My name is Jody Chapman," Jody said. "I'm looking for my brother Michael. He's fourteen. I have a picture."

151

"There's a coffee shop across the street," Frankie said. "Why don't we go there and talk?"

"All right," Jody said. "But you'll look at his picture there?"

Frankie nodded. "Come on, we got the light," he said, and taking Jody's arm, he jogged across the street.

They found a booth and sat down opposite each other. The air conditioning was on full blast, and Jody shivered as her body cooled off. It felt good though, and it felt great to put her bag down. "Here's Michael's picture," Jody said, handing it to Frankie. "The picture is a year old, so he's probably grown since then."

Frankie examined the picture carefully. "Fourteen?" he said.

Jody nodded. "He'll be fifteen next month."

"And you think he's in New York?"

"I don't know," Jody said. "You don't recognize him?"

Frankie shook his head. "Never saw him before."

The waitress came over and asked for their order. Frankie asked for a diet Coke, and Jody ordered the same.

"I have to watch my weight," Frankie said. "Nobody likes a fat boy."

"Oh," Jody said. "Look, Frankie, if you don't know Michael, do you know somebody who might?"

"How long have you been in New York?" Frankie asked.

"Ten minutes," Jody said. "Give or take."

"Give or take," Frankie said. "I'm sorry, I forgot your name."

"Jody," she replied. "Jody Chapman."

"Jody, go back home," Frankie said. "Believe me, if your brother's been here for a year, then he doesn't want to get found."

"How can you know?" Jody said. "He's just a kid."

"He's older than I am," Frankie said. "I won't be fifteen until Thanksgiving."

"You're kidding," Jody said. "You look so much older."

"Listen to me, okay," Frankie said. "I don't know where your brother is and I don't know why he ran away. But unless things are really rotten at home, go back there and go back there soon. I bet you don't even have a place to stay tonight."

Jody shook her head. "I thought I'd spend the night looking for Michael," she replied. "I know he might be on the streets."

"You don't know anything," Frankie declared. "Look, a couple of years ago my mother told me to pack my bags and get out, I was slowing her down. So I hitched my way to New York and I've been here ever since. I earn my money turning tricks because there's nothing else a fourteen-year-old can do. No one'll hire you for a real job. And it's okay. I'll do it for as long as I have to, until I have enough money saved up to move to Hollywood and become an actor. I've already done some porn work, so I know I can get jobs. But I want to be a real actor, you know, like on TV."

Jody nodded.

"I'm real photogenic," Frankie continued. "That means I photograph good. And I don't do too many drugs, 'cause they can really ruin your looks. I know a hundred guys just like me. I'm better-looking than most of them, but we all do the same stuff, make the same rounds, so to speak. A hundred, maybe more, and we're just the ones who hang out around the New Apollo. Lots of other guys hang out in front of lots of other theaters and that's just in Manhattan. There's a lot of action in Brooklyn too, and Queens."

The waitress brought them their soft drinks. Frankie took a long sip out of his.

"Most of the guys are pretty heavy into drugs," Frankie said. "Some deal, they all buy. Some of the boys who don't hustle work for dealers. There are hundreds of them too, probably thousands. I know maybe ten. If your brother's dealing drugs, there's no way you'd ever find him."

"Michael wouldn't do that," Jody said.

"You think he'd sell his body instead?" Frankie asked.

"I don't know what I think," Jody admitted.

"Listen, you come to the city to try to find your brother, and that's really sweet," Frankie said. "I guess you figured he was just hanging out here for a year, sleeping on subways, stealing food out of garbage cans. And if he is in New York, that's probably how he started. That's how I started, I know. But after a while garbage doesn't taste so good anymore and you want to sleep in a bed again and you do what you have to to make money. Nobody lives in New York for a year sleeping on subways. A month, maybe two, but then you start hustling. And once you do that you can't ever go back home. No matter what home was like, it isn't there for you anymore. You don't need it. When you're stealing garbage, home always looks good. When you're earning money, the New Apollo is your home. You understand?"

"But what if Michael wants to be found?" Jody said.

"There are halfway houses," Frankie replied. "And hot lines for kids who decide to call home. A lot of kids take one look at the scene and realize they'll never survive here. They turn around and go right home, or they try someplace else, some smaller city where there's less action and it's less scary. Your brother could have done that. He could have come to New York and then moved on to Philly or Boston. You gonna go looking for him in every city in America?"

Jody shook her head.

"You sure he's even alive?" Frankie asked.

"No," Jody whispered.

"I don't think he ran away," Frankie said. "If I had a sister who cared enough about me to come looking, I never would have run away."

"If he didn't run away, then he's probably dead," Jody said.

"If he did run away, then he might as well be dead," Frankie replied. "Jody, go on home. Give me that picture of Michael, and write your number on it. If I ever see him, I'll give you a call. I promise. I like you, Jody. I wish I'd had a sister like you. Go home before you get into trouble you can't handle."

"You can call collect," Jody said. "You will call if you see him?"

"Promise," Frankie said. "Now pay for these sodas and I'll go back to work. It's Saturday night, there're a lot of guys looking for me."

"I hope you become a big star," Jody said.

"Sure," he replied. "Frankie Goes to Hollywood." He took the picture from Jody and smiled.

"Thank you," Jody said.

"You know how to get back to Port Authority?" Frankie asked.

"It's down a couple of blocks," Jody said. "The big building on the right."

"You got it," Frankie said. "Take care, Jody. And I hope you find out about Michael." He stuffed the picture in his pocket and sauntered out of the coffee shop.

Jody paid for the sodas and walked the two blocks back. The streets were teeming with people. She looked at all the boys talking to men, saw the exchange of smiles, the exchange of money. None of the boys were Michael. She wondered how many of them had parents, sisters, brothers, grandparents, all sick with worry about where they had gone to. She wondered if Michael was one of them, and she wondered, as she always did, if she would ever find out.

The next bus going home was at eight in the morning. Jody found she was too restless and too scared to wait at Port Authority all that time. So she walked out of the building and began wandering the neighborhood. She had money for a cab back and many hours to kill.

After walking for several blocks, not really caring which direction she was going in, Jody found herself in a residential neighborhood, a quiet section of blocks without lurid movie marquees and dirty book stores. Even the air felt cooler where she was, and Jody could feel herself relax. There were couples holding hands, people walking their dogs, even some kids playing on the sidewalks. Jody looked at all of them and wished that Kay was with her. She missed Kay, she realized, more than she would have thought possible. She missed Kay even more than she missed Michael, even though she knew where Kay was, and could always call her if she really wanted to talk. But Kay had been there for that year, been there when Michael wasn't, and Jody needed her now, needed Kay to repeat to her all the things that Frankie had said about how Michael was lost forever and there was no point trying to find him.

Jody realized she was about to start crying, and she couldn't bear the thought of doing it in public in New York City. She looked around for a building to go into, and saw one. Its name was The Ninth Avenue Church and its door was open, and that was all the invitation she needed.

Jody walked in. There were a few people sitting in the pews, praying. Jody found an empty row in the back, put her bag down, and began to weep.

"Can I help you?"

Jody looked up and saw the person speaking to her was a minister.

"I'm sorry," she said. "I'll go now."

"No," the minister said. "Please don't. I just wanted to know if I could help."

"I'm looking for my brother," Jody said. "I have a picture. His name is Michael Chapman and he's fourteen, and he's been missing for almost a year."

"I see," the minister said. "Do you know he's in New York?"

"No," Jody said. "I just came to look for him, and I'm never going to find him. I'm going home tomorrow morning. You haven't seen him, have you?"

"No," the minister replied. "My name is Bruce Richards. I don't believe you told me yours."

"Jody," Jody said. "Jody Chapman. My brother's name is Michael."

"Have you heard from him at all this past year?" Reverend Richards asked.

Jody shook her head. "He just vanished," she said. "He was going to play softball at his friend's house and we never saw him again. My sister Kay thinks he's dead. She's twelve."

"Your family has really suffered," Reverend Richards said. "Did Kay come with you on this search?"

"She's in Florida with my grandparents," Jody said. "Mom kicked her out. They've all really gone crazy." Jody began crying again.

Reverend Richards sat by her side saying nothing until Jody got herself under control. He gave her his handkerchief, which she used gratefully, then handed back to him.

"I'm sorry," Jody said.

"You have nothing to apologize for," he told her.

"I was stupid to come to New York," Jody said. "I just feel so helpless. I needed to do something. All year long I've been doing things, trying to figure out where Michael might be, and trying to keep my family together, and all I've done is fail. We have no idea where Michael is, and I don't think we're ever going to find out. And my parents, well, they were only staying

156

together for our sake anyway, and now Michael is missing, and Kay's in Florida, and I'll be going to college in a year, so why should they stay together? They'll get a divorce and even if Michael does come back, things will never be the same." She began to cry again, but only for a moment.

"Do your parents know where you are?" Reverend Richards asked.

"It's okay," Jody said. "They think I'm staying with a friend. They won't be worrying about me. I don't think they have any worry left in them anyway. And I'll be home tomorrow afternoon."

"You can call them," he said.

"It's better if I don't," Jody replied. "Honest."

"Well, you can't spend the night at Port Authority," he said.

"It's okay," Jody said. "I'm not going to sleep tonight anyway. All I've done this summer is sleep. I can last for one night without any."

"You can stay in my office," he said. "We lock up the building at ten, but I'll come back tomorrow morning around six and open up for you."

"Thank you," Jody said. "I'd like to spend the night in a church. I haven't been going lately, and it's something I've been missing."

"Has your minister been able to help you?" Reverend Richards asked.

"He's tried," Jody said. "Everybody's tried. I've heard a lot about suffering and a lot about faith, but none of it has really helped. There really isn't any help."

"I wish you didn't feel that way," he said.

"Kay hopes he's dead," Jody said. "So there'd be an end to it. You don't know what it's like, living in a void. We can't forget Michael, because there's always the chance he'll walk right through the door. And we can't keep hoping, because there's always the chance he's dead. It's gotten to the point where all we can do is hate. Hate and not feel and wish it was all over."

"Have you tried praying?" he asked.

"Of course I have," Jody said. "First I prayed for Michael, and then I prayed for an answer, and then I just prayed for enough strength to make it through the day. God doesn't hear me."

"He hears," Reverend Richards said. "Perhaps you can't hear Him."

"I'm too tired to argue theology," Jody said, stretching. "I know you mean well. Everyone means well, but nobody knows the right thing to say."

"What is the right thing to say?" he asked.

"David Templeton," Jody replied, almost smiling.

"What?" Reverend Richards asked.

"David Templeton," Jody said. "There's this boy Jerry, he was Michael's best friend, and I found him crying on the first day of school. God, that was a long time ago. Anyway, he was crying and I was afraid he'd get me crying, so I made up this signal. David Templeton. It's just the name of a kid in his class, but if either of us thought we were going to start crying again, we'd think 'David Templeton' to ourselves and then we wouldn't cry. It worked for Jerry at least. I never saw him cry again. I guess he got over Michael being gone. But I need some words just like David Templeton, only words that mean something. Something I can say to myself when I'm home and I realize everything is just in shambles because Kay's gone and Michael's still missing and my mother's crazy and my father's a failure. I need a David Templeton. I don't suppose you know any words like that."

"David Templeton," Reverend Richards said thoughtfully. "Let me think."

"I'd really appreciate it," Jody said. "I worry sometimes that I'm going to start screaming and never be able to stop. I almost did that once, only it was laughing, and even that my boyfriend couldn't handle. But the thing is, I still love my family. Kay's been impossible for months now, and I still love her, and my mother's been awful, and I love her, and my father, well, he's hardly a father anymore, but I love him anyway, and in spite of it all, I still love Michael. So I don't want to start screaming. I know things will never be good again, but if I start screaming then things will only get worse, and I don't want that either. I need an antiscreaming prayer."

"I think I have one," Reverend Richards said. "It's from Corinthians, and it's helped me over some rough spots. Want to hear?"

"Sure," Jody said.

" 'Love bears all things, believes all things, hopes all things, endures all things. Love never ends.' " He spoke the words slowly. "What do you think?"

"I like it," Jody said. "I didn't know the Bible talked that much about love."

"It's *charity* in the King James version," he said. "They've retranslated it to love."

"How does it go again?" Jody asked. "I'd like to memorize it."

"Tell you what," he said. "Let's go into my office and I'll write it down for you. And you can give me that picture of Michael. I'll put it up on our bulletin board so our parishioners can be on the lookout for him. All right?"

"Fine," Jody said, following him out of the chapel. "Thank you for everything."

"I hope I've been of help," he said. "Here, let me write it down for you." He took out a piece of paper from his desk and wrote the words down.

" 'Love bears all things, believes all things, hopes all things, endures all things,' " Jody read when he finished. " 'Love never ends.' Ain't that the truth."

"It sure is," he said, and he took Jody's hand and held it gently between his own. "Jody, listen to me. None of what's happened is your responsibility."

"You mean Michael's disappearing?" Jody asked. "I know that's not my fault."

"That's not what I mean," he said. "I mean all the rest of it, your parents' problems with your sister, their marriage, their inability to cope. You're not the little Dutch boy with his finger in the dike. You're just a kid yourself, and no matter how hard you try, you're not going to be able to solve everyone's problems single-handedly. There's no reason for you to even try."

"But if I don't, who will?" Jody asked.

"Maybe your mother will," Reverend Richards said. "Maybe your father. Maybe things are beyond solving, and you're going to have to spend the next few years of your life learning how to cope with the changes. I can't predict the future. But I've never known a child to keep her parents' marriage together, and I've certainly never known a child to salvage an entire family. It just doesn't work that way, and if you can realize that, and deal with it, then I think things might get a little better for you."

"I know I've been trying too much," Jody said. "But lately I've been trying too little."

"It's not a question of trying too much or too little," Reverend Richards said. "It's trying the right things that counts. Like getting good grades, and not leaving home without permission, and learning to accept your family as is."

" 'As is' is pretty bad these days," Jody said.

"I don't doubt it," Reverend Richards replied. "The trick is to try not to make it even worse."

Jody smiled at him. "I like the idea of not being responsible for everything," she said. "It almost sounds like a vacation."

Reverend Richards smiled back at her and pointed to the couch in his office. "Get some sleep, Jody," he said. "I'll see you in the morning."

"Thank you," she said. "For everything." She watched as he left his office, and she found she felt more at peace than she had in a long, long time. When she was sure she was alone, she read the sheet of paper with the magic words on it again and again, until she had them committed to memory, until they had lulled her to sleep.

Sunday, August 3

"Jody, my God, where were you?"

"I was at Maris's aunt's," Jody replied. "I've only been gone since yesterday. What's the big deal?"

"We know you weren't at Maris's aunt's," her father replied. "Come on in. We've been worried sick."

Jody shook her head in disgust. "How did you find out?" she asked.

"I ran into Lauren this morning," her mother said. "And I mentioned where you were, and Lauren told me you couldn't possibly be there because she saw Maris out on a date last night. We called Maris's aunt and she said she hadn't seen either of you, and we've been trying to reach Maris all day but there hasn't been an answer and we thought, oh, I don't even want to say what we thought. Are you all right?"

"I'm fine, Mom," Jody said. "I went to New York City to look for Michael. Only I didn't find him and I realized I wasn't going to, so I came home. The last thing I wanted was for you to worry."

"I even called Florida," her mother said. "To see if Kay knew where you were."

"How's Kay?" Jody asked.

"The same," her mother said. "Oh, I don't know. Maybe she isn't. Maybe none of us are anymore."

"You'd better call her back to tell her I'm all right," Jody said. "Kay worries a lot more than you think."

"Don't ever lie to us again," her father said. "Jody, we need the truth from you, no matter what it is."

"Sure, Dad," Jody said. "I'm sorry."

"We were worried sick," he continued. "We thought maybe you'd heard something about Michael and were too scared to tell us. We thought Kay had sent for you and you'd left us for her. We thought lots of things and they were all ugly and frightening."

"I really am sorry," Jody said. "I thought what I was doing was right, but it wasn't. I never meant to scare you."

"Maybe it's a good thing you did," he said. "There was a moment there when I thought I had lost all three of my children. I can't possibly describe what that felt like."

"Tom," Jody's mother said.

"No, listen to me," Jody's father said. "We're not living like this anymore, shattered and fragmented. I don't know what can be salvaged anymore, but we're going to try."

"How?" Jody's mother asked. "Michael is lost."

"Kay isn't," Jody's father replied. "And you're not, and I'm not, and thank God, Jody isn't either. Kay's going to start the school year here, and we're going to go into family therapy and see if we can find the love I know we all used to have for each other. Maybe it'll just prove to be another disaster, but we have to try."

"Oh, Dad," Jody said.

"I'm scared," Jody's mother said. "It scares me, Tom."

"We need help, Linda," Jody's father said. "We've tried doing it on our own, and we can't. You know that. You stared into the same abyss I did today. You know the only way we can have a future together is if we get help."

"I know," Jody's mother said, and she took a deep breath. "Sometimes I don't want to, but I know. Well, I guess I'd better start by calling Kay again." She walked over to the phone, and with trembling fingers pressed the numbers.

"Hello, Kay," she said. "Kay, Jody's back. Yes, she's fine. She went looking for Michael. Yes, we're glad too. We're very glad. Hold on, Kay, I'll put Jody on. And Kay. Kay, I love you very much."

Jody looked at her house, her parents, the phone that had suddenly become a new, hopeful connection to her sister. " 'Love bears all things, believes all things, hopes all things, endures all things,' " she thought to herself. " 'Love never ends.' David Templeton." She took the phone from her mother and said, "Hi, Kay. What's up?"

*H*e's been gone one week short of a year now; it's been a year without Michael. I wake up each morning no longer expecting to see him, but at least Kay is home now, and knowing that helps me face each day.

Sometimes at night when I can't sleep I go into their bedrooms just to feel their presence. I go to Kay's first, and look at her surrounded by the handful of teddy bears she allowed herself to keep after she turned twelve. Her breathing is deep and steady, and while her hands are half clenched in fists there is a peacefulness to her that promises hope. And then seeing Kay back home gives me the strength I need to face Michael's things.

I tiptoe down the hall and enter his room quietly, so that I won't wake Mom up. She sleeps lightly now, and when she can't sleep she goes to his empty bedroom also. It startles her to find me here, so I make as little noise as possible.

I open Michael's closet door first and find his presents still waiting for him, the computer, the baseball card book, even Kay's rock. All as neatly gift-wrapped as they were on Christmas.

Then I go through his drawers, taking out his shirts, his underwear, his socks. I hold them to my cheek, trying to catch the last lingering remnants of his scent.

I put them back where I found them, because Mom will be doing the same things later, and then I pick up the notebooks he'd bought for school and never used, all those bright, shiny, appropriate-for-high-school notebooks. They sit on his desk, waiting for him. Everything in Michael's room waits for him.

I feel him very strongly in there sometimes, the Michael I will always remember. Sometimes he's just a little kid, crying as he falls, losing his first tooth, reading out loud, tossing a softball. Sometimes he's Michael as he was when he left, promising he won't be late for dinner. That was the last thing I heard Michael say, that he wouldn't be late for dinner. How very silly.

I let the memories of Michael wash over me. I conjure up his

163

images, the littlest Michael, the funniest Michael, the sweetest Michael that I can remember. And I feel full of love for him then, nothing else, just the love a sister feels for her brother, a love that endures all things and never ends. I love my brother, whatever has become of him, whatever he's become. My love for Michael burns steady in those moments, and it illuminates my life.

I lie on Michael's bed for a while, looking up at the ceiling, feeling his mattress support me the way it supported him, and then I get up, knowing I still won't sleep, but starting to feel like a trespasser. I straighten his bedspread out, pick up his notebooks, touch his socks, check out his presents, gaze all around his room, looking at all the things that once belonged to Michael, that once were part of Michael.

I look around at all those things and I know that's all they are, just Michael's things in his bedroom. Books and clothes and gifts and bedspread, but there is no Michael. There is no Michael.

ABOUT THE AUTHOR

SUSAN BETH PFEFFER graduated from New York University with a major in television, motion pictures, and radio. She is a native New Yorker and now lives in Middletown, New York. She is the author of many acclaimed young adult novels, including *About David, Fantasy Summer, Getting Even, Starring Peter and Leigh,* as well as the popular series *Make Me a Star.*

S000 464

F
PFE*FFER* Pfeffer, Susan Beth

The year without
Michael

87-11474

DATE DUE
